Edward Maitland

The Pilgrim and the Shrine

Or passages from the life and correspondence of Herert Ainslie. Vol. 3

Edward Maitland

The Pilgrim and the Shrine
Or passages from the life and correspondence of Herert Ainslie. Vol. 3

ISBN/EAN: 9783337292195

Printed in Europe, USA, Canada, Australia, Japan

Cover: Foto ©Andreas Hilbeck / pixelio.de

More available books at **www.hansebooks.com**

THE

PILGRIM AND THE SHRINE;

OR,

PASSAGES FROM THE LIFE AND CORRESPONDENCE

OF

HERBERT AINSLIE, B.A.,

CANTAB.

'I have always contended that obedience even to an erring conscience was
the way to gain light, and that it mattered not where a man began so that he
began on what came to hand, and in faith; and that anything might become a
divine method of truth; that to the pure all things are pure, and have a self-
correcting virtue and power of germinating.'—NEWMAN's 'Apologia,' p. 333.
　　　　　'He faced the spectres of the mind,
　　　　　　And laid them.'
　　　　　'At last he beat his music out.'
　　　　　　　　　TENNYSON'S ' In Memoriam.'

IN THREE VOLUMES.—VOL. II.

LONDON:
TINSLEY BROTHERS, 18, CATHERINE ST., STRAND.
1868.

CONTENTS

OF

THE SECOND VOLUME.

BOOK III. *continued.*

BOOK IV.

CONTENTS.

BOOK V.

BOOK VI.

BOOK III. *continued.*

CHAPTER VI.

A DISAPPOINTMENT.

HERBERT does not restrict his chances of making a fortune to his own personal operations. Extensive preparations have been made by companies of miners for turning the neighbouring river out of its bed at various points.

The wealth found in the banks has raised sanguine expectations that the bed

will prove enormously rich, and many a
miner has embarked the whole of his earnings in the venture.   At a great price
Herbert has obtained shares in some of
these undertakings.   The skill and energy
displayed by the Americans, the manner
in which, with so few appliances, they
compel the wilderness to minister to their
wants, strike him as most admirable.
Huge trees are felled, and sawn into
planks, and shot down into the steep cañ-
ons of the river.   Long wooden channels,
by them called 'Flumes,' are constructed,
and strong dams are made to turn the
whole of the water into them.   At length,
after several months of hard work, and
impatient waiting for the water to fall
sufficiently low, the bed is laid dry.   Alas
for those who had been eagerly looking
forward to spending next Christmas in
the home to which their fortunate venture
shall have brought affluence and comfort.

Instead of the bed of clay glittering throughout with scales and lumps of gold, nought appears but bare granite, smooth and polished by the ceaseless rushing of the waters. It is thus in every case in which Herbert is interested. His prospect of leaving California with a competence is indefinitely postponed, and his sanguine temperament feels the disappointment keenly. But to many the shock is more than they can bear. To most dispositions adversity is more demoralizing than prosperity. While one class of miners at once seek fresh scenes of labour, reckless drunkenness is the resource of others; and one poor fellow takes refuge in suicide.

Herbert went over to the settlement the Sunday after the failure was declared. He finds the men all lounging listlessly about, not knowing what to do next, and not sufficiently recovered from the shock to feel energy for anything; so enormous is the amount of labour thrown away, and so high have hopes been raised. A little interest is awakened by the arrival of a preacher, of whom Herbert has already heard from his men, who comes to deliver his usual weekly discourse. Herbert listens with the rest. Strange, it strikes him, is the clinging to dogma and the ignoring of the heart's real feelings, which mark most preachers of all denominations. This man, a shrewd genial man enough in his ordinary life, no sooner begins to teach others than he begins to say what he does not feel, and cannot really believe. Why will preachers think that inhuman sentiments cease to be inhuman and become divine if uttered in a sermon? Herbert gets angry when in attempting to 'improve' the incident of the poor suicide, the preacher finds no pity or sympathy, but only denunciation. 'For filthy lucre.'

He waits until it is over, and then

while all are listening, he asks how he knew that 'poor Harry had rushed un-bidden into the presence of his Maker?'

'Why, didn't he shoot himself?'

'Yes, but how are you and I to know that that was not the very mode in which his Maker desired him to appear before him? Had life been reft from him by ill-ness or accident, you would have regarded these as ministers of God to do his will; what less claim have the circumstances which drove him to this deed, and the nature upon which they so acted, to be considered divinely ordained? He did not make his own sensitive disposition, or cause his own disappointment.'

'Then you don't condemn him for put-ting an end to himself?'

'It is not my business to condemn any-body. I only think that if he could have looked forward two or three years, he would have found his future self saying how foolish he was to take his disappointment so much to heart. At that distance of time the whole matter will seem a small one.'

Some of the miners thank him afterwards for that last remark. 'It is bad enough now, but they guess they won't care so much about it after a bit, if they can only hold on till then.'

A few days, and all are busy again on new ground, hope revives, and misfortunes are forgotten. So runs the gold-hunter's life. Fascinating in its uncertainty as that of the gambler, but without the demoralization; the hard labour saves it from that, and still more the consciousness that the success of one is not the ruin of another.—At nobody's expense save that of mother earth, and she is willing enough.

Herbert himself will have soon to seek other scenes of labour, for not only is his present claim nearly worked out, but the supply of water is rapidly failing. He feels much regret at the prospect of quitting that neighbourhood, for he has had many pleasant experiences there. His intercourse with his neighbours, rough and unlettered though they are, has taught him to form a higher estimate altogether of individuals; not perhaps of their wisdom or moral excellence, but he has learnt thoroughly to discard the carefully inculcated notion of the total depravity of everybody. And, as some of the notes made before quitting this spot will show, he thinks he has succeeded in discovering how it is that men accept a belief so contrary both to reason and to experience. He writes :—

'As the tendency of a wound is to heal, so the general bias of human nature seems to be towards good.

'I have found that the miners when they have come to borrow any of my few books, have generally asked for "some-thing true." The country is inundated with novels, mostly translations from the French, lively and clever, but of low rank in the scale of morals. But even these have in several instances served a good end, for they have attracted many to read who would otherwise never have looked into a book. These highly-seasoned ro-mances have served to awaken many a torpid intellect to a sense of its powers. Once awakened, the mind soon finds that such food cloys without nourishing, and demands something more satisfactory. The habit of reading and the desire for know-ledge once formed, the transition is easy and natural to more useful knowledge. At least, many of these practical back-woods'-men have found it so. The only question they ask when borrowing of me is, " Is it true ?"

' If indeed the mind remains satisfied

with light or low reading; if the individual sinks into a mere novel reader, it is probably a proof, not of the necessarily bad effects of such literature, but of the mental imbecility of the individual. Such an one would never have done any good. I confess that to myself it is an immense delight and relaxation to get hold of one of Dumas' exciting novels. For many an hour of pleasant and wholesome refreshment am I indebted to "Monte Christo," and the wonderful series which begins with the "Three Musketeers." Perhaps these hardly deserve the name of light reading. There is an element of grandeur in them that places them far higher in the scale. The death of poor Porthos is itself an epic, and truly Homeric. And the picture of a man making himself a providence and a fate to others is not unsuggestive of a moral.

'I am sure it is a great mistake to condemn whatever is not adapted to the highest parts of our nature, or the most advanced stages of its development. And it is a mistake constantly made by those who ignore the fact that man has many sides to his nature, and that the lower are as necessary a part of him as the higher.

'Not to those who most need it is the gospel preached, but to the select few who already have, or pretend to, a lofty spirituality, such as the mass of mankind are quite unable to comprehend. Calling themselves the elect, they hold that the "scheme of salvation" was contrived only for them, and complacently regard everybody without their little circle as reprobate. How completely does any miscellaneous assemblage of men give the lie to these notions. Among the crowd upon a race-course at home, or in the ship that brought me here, or with these miners, it is impossible not to feel that some far larger theory of God and of the meaning of the universe must be adopted if it is to be applicable to more than one out of many thousands of the human race. How many a clergyman have I known in England who shuts himself up to the society of a select few who flatter and humour him, and consult him about delicate mental, or rather emotional, phenomena, and mutually flatter each other into believing that they are the saints, and abandon all who remain without their little coterie to the "uncovenanted mercies of God," but never venture among them for fear of having to enlarge their theory and lessen their own complacency. It is so pleasant to think ourselves the special objects of divine favour; and so hard to believe in injustice when our own merits are so fully recognized.

'The poor Major's library consisted of a cookery book and a Bible. An American, seeing the latter in my hut the other day, remarked, " Excellent work that; there are some first-rate things in it."

'I envied him his frame of mind, it was so evidently free from any slavish superstition or prejudice. Truly in its simple narratives may be found a complete revelation of *man*. In it he is drawn in all the extent of his nature, without the alteration of a single feature. From the lowest depths to the loftiest attainments of which he is capable, from Ahab to Jesus, all degrees are represented there. It is a gallery in which all the pictures are life-like; but the subjects are so varied that none are too gross for admission. A revelation of God is impossible to our faculties, but the Bible reveals man's idea of God in the various stages of its growth. It consequently represents Him under characters as widely different as were the men themselves who recorded their conceptions; from the "jealous," unscrupulous, Jewish patriot-God Jehovah, to the universal loving Father. Men cannot imagine God to be other than that which they themselves appreciate. A " revelation of God," therefore, is a revelation, not of God, but of man, inasmuch as man's ideal is the index to his own character.'

/ L

CHAPTER VII.

PROGRESS.

HERBERT's chief delight is in his meditations among the pine trees. He is wandering farther and farther from the tracks of his youth. He has got into a world of thought so wide that he can nowhere dash himself against its boundaries; out of the concrete into the abstract. The predominant sensation is one of joy. Like an escaped captive just free from his prison and his chains, he hardly knows yet whither to betake himself. The joy of being free is enough for the present. Why hurry to a conclusion? All things are progressive. If there is the infinite to be studied, there is eternity for the task. Why not linger among the delights of the road?

Something has been gained of late; for he no longer feels in danger of being overwhelmed by the deep waters in which he is floating. He no longer requires to touch the bottom in order to spring up. He feels that in the very ocean around him is ever-present the universal Divinity, as much as in any other place. And so he writes, ' There is no nucleus of Deity; God being infinite, his centre must be everywhere. He is here, above, below, and around; where the two infinities of earth and sky, like life and death, ever kiss each other, as much here as in the un-attainable abyss.' And again, ' There is no absolute, no perfection. All things must be progressive. Does progression

necessarily involve termini ? or can we
have any idea of progression in the infinite ?   Yet, had absolute perfection
existed prior to the "creation," the universe
had never been.   For why create, unless
to produce a state of things better than
before existed ?   For the greater glory of
God ?   Then His glory was capable of increase, and therefore was not complete.
Therefore there was no perfection ; therefore no God !   Into this maze of contradic-
tion do the theologians lead us, by detach-
ing God from the universe, and making
Him a being apart.   Abolish degrees in
anything, and it vanishes altogether.   The
only absolute is annihilation.   In evil, it
must destroy itself and vanish.   In perfection also it is absolute nothingness.

'A condition in which there are no
degrees and no contrasts is a condition of
negation.   All light would be no light.
All goodness would be no goodness.   No

distance can be great absolutely, but only as compared with a less distance. It is the imperfection necessary to the finite that theologians confound with sin. Hence comes their doctrine of the total depravity of human nature. They mistake imperfection for wickedness. Existence is a scale whose extremes are infinitely distant, for it may be divided into degrees infinitely small. All things are somewhere between those two extremes. In any condition of existence whatever, however high and excellent, however low and base, it is possible for those dwelling there to conceive something still better, still worse. Let us be placed where we may we can still see a Beyond. Those who have won the highest place in heaven itself have only won the ability to perceive something far higher and better towards which they may aspire. They have only enlarged the circle of their desires, and their actual place is one with which they are dissatisfied, and which they long to transcend. The popular idea of perfection necessitates the power to imagine a worse, but none to imagine a better, state of being. The distance from God will ever seem the greatest to those who have the highest faculties for appreciating Him. The highest in heaven will thus feel themselves the lowest. They may even thus feel themselves so far from God that heaven will be no heaven to them; and they may have less pleasure in existence than the tenants of hell itself. For in order to exist continuously in any place the nature of the individual must harmonize to such a degree with the conditions of the place as to derive a certain satisfaction from the mere fulfilling of those conditions. Unmitigated suffering, therefore, cannot long exist. There must be some degree of satisfaction; some pleasure wherever there is life. Hell is defined to be a state of separation from God. But, as appears above, this is a condition of which the tenants of heaven are better able to appreciate the evil. So that even these dread extremes meet, and heaven and hell are one!

'A simple statement, however, disposes of the orthodox tenet on this head. The principles of our nature must ever be our guide. We can imagine no good being to be perfectly happy while any are hopelessly wretched. If there is a hell, therefore, there can be no heaven. If a heaven, no hell. The ideas are of necessity mutually destructive. What St Augustine wrote to the contrary was written by him as a theologian, not as a man. And truly inhuman was a theology which could make the contemplation of the torments of the damned one of the principal delights of the saved. This earth, indeed, may comprise the elements of both in itself.

If a condition of hopeful progress towards the loftiest end be the happiest possible for intelligent beings, surely there are many such in this world, and to them it is indeed a heaven. If remorse and hopelessness be the lot of the most miserable, there are those who find their hell here. The vast majority are between these extremes. The question for them is to which do they tend? Whereabouts on the infinite ladder am I, and in which direction do I tend? I know no man who can tell me, and I have none to guide me aright if I tend awrong; none but the instincts of my nature, and the influence of the things that surround me. Is more vouchsafed to any? Have any a right to demand more; to require an infallible guide that shall supersede all necessity of exertion and watchfulness on their part? Out upon the old notions that would detach me from the Universe of which I am a part, and send me wandering through space in search of a distinct, isolated, impossible God! No, no: the Universe is Alive, and He is its Life: " The Life of the world." O ye trees, living columns in these sombre aisles, be not incommunicable to me who seek to learn from you. Reveal to me the mystery of your own being, and perchance I shall discover the secret of mine. Answer for me the question that haunts me; for of late, wherever I have turned my steps, whether busy at my work, or following with my gun in the tracks of the stag, or wrapped in my blanket at night, the question hath continually rung in my ears : ' What is thine end and aim ?' And I am disquieted in my mind, for I cannot answer it. I seem to myself to be no more than yon lizard that dies after a life spent in the pursuit and digestion of insects. Or even as yourselves, who, after contending for a few seasons with the blasts, fall and become a prey to the fires of the wild man, and whiten the ground with your ashes. What do I here? and what do ye here? Do ye, like some of us men, work, and wonder, and add to your wonder worship? or do ye, like other of us, simply enjoy without thinking or even being conscious of it? I see much that ye may enjoy; in the air, and the light, and the moisture; in the shedding your pollen for a future generation, and in protecting your slender pinelings, and the flowers that grow between. But is this all?

'And it seemed to me that in the murmur of the breeze through their topmost branches, they sighed down for answer, "We follow the impulse of our nature. The deeper we strike our roots into earth, the higher we rise towards heaven." '

CHAPTER VIII.

A HAPPY FAMILY.

It is of no use to remain longer where
he is. So, previous to making a fresh start,
Herbert visits the Bay. He there finds letters from home, exhibiting mingled feelings of anxiety for his health and safety in
that wild land, and mortification at his de-
sertion of his profession, tempered, however, by half-suppressed satisfaction at his
prospects of success, which Herbert now
fears he may have drawn in too bright
colours. For the time his chronic home-
sickness is checked; not that his affection

is in any way diminished, but letters and papers from a place we know often seem to transport us thither, in such a measure as to satisfy our longing to be there. From the poor Major's family, also, he receives the warmest acknowledgment of his care and friendship for their lost relative, with an urgent request that he will accept the money made by him in California. They feel that Herbert has a 'better claim to it than anybody else, for they are certain the poor fellow would never have made a sixpence by himself.' These two or three hundred pounds, for it does not appear to have been more, make a welcome addition to Herbert's little capital; and the kindly tone of the communication produces a glow of pleasure that he feels a sufficient compensation for much hardship.

He enjoys this visit to the city more than any previous one. It is getting more settled and civilized. Indeed, in no respect, save in position, is it the same city. For San Francisco has been burnt down two or three times of late. The canvas city gave place to a wooden one; and the wooden city has given place to one of brick, and stone, and iron. He meets people whose society is pleasant to him. There are many women and children now dwelling there, and a child's cry is to him the sweetest music, after his sojourn in the wilderness. School-houses and churches are beginning to rear their heads. With one of the latter he seems specially pleased, for it is the joint property of three different sects, who have united their means to build it, agreeing to use it in turn at different times of the day. He becomes intimate with a New England family, all the members of which are occupied in the same business, but belong to different sects; one or more of them attending each of the services in the joint-stock chapel. Herbert notes that on most ordinary topics, on all affecting their personal relations in life, they are agreed, but on Sunday they diverge each to his own communion, and meet at the supper-table in the evening in harmony so perfect and natural that he cannot but contrast with it the bitterness and gloom that such difference of opinion would engender in every family of his acquaintance in England. Speaking of this one day to the father, a homely square-built man, full of strong good sense, he answered: 'I guess now, in the old country your fathers there just want their children to look upon them as possessing popish infallibility, and so won't let them have any mind of their own. Now, you see, if I was to begin with my youngsters in that way, our Yankee children are so keen that they would soon find out that I was no more infallible than they are.

And when they found me pretending to be what I ain't really, they would set me down as a humbug. I can't stand that, so I let them know the first thing that I have only been in the world a trifle longer than themselves, just enough to get a class or two above them in the big school. That I'll tell them all I know, and the more they can find out for themselves the better. I do my best. I teach them to be more afraid of doing wrong than of offending me; but I don't set up for a pattern for them in thinking, any more than I do in looks. Some of them take after me, and some after their mother. You ought to have known that woman. Such a right down clever one, and so fond of me,— often said she wouldn't take ten thousand dollars for me. Well, if they ain't all alike in looks, I don't see why they should be all alike in their ways of thinking. There's Amos, there, he's death on punkins, and he keeps healthy and strong on 'em, while they knock me right down if I just touch the least morsel. Well, our minds differ just about as much, but we are none the worse friends for that. I guess your old country fathers go on a different sort of tack; but I reckon they haven't got a better set of boys than mine.'

Sometimes the supper is enlivened by a comparison of the various discourses they have heard during the day, and a discussion about their respective doctrines, but always in perfect charity, as if each one felt that though his belief was the best for him, yet it was not necessarily so for the others. The only approach to bigotry is on the part of an uncle, who sometimes joins the party; a hard-featured descendant of the Puritans, and who still clings to their rigid faith and practice. His presence is generally the signal for a dog-

matic turn to the conversation. Of an ascetic temperament, he looked with great
distrust on all who gave any scope to their
natural capacity for enjoyment. He could
not understand how a person could fre-
quent theatres and other places of amusement, and yet be a sincere Christian, with
hope in the future. He loved to dilate on
what he had read about the evil of such
places, the temptations and light company,
especially of the theatre. He was thankful that he had never tempted Providence
by going thither; but he knew enough by
description to cause him to fear greatly for
those who did go. It was to such a tirade
that one of the party, a young man whose
eye and brow bespoke him an artist of no
mean order, made answer:

'My uncle, I never lose a chance of
going to the theatre when there is to be a
good representation; but I know nothing
of the things whereof you seem to have

heard so much. No doubt there is evil everywhere for those who look out for it, but not necessarily in a theatre any more than in a church. I go to enjoy the lofty language of the poet, and the actor's delineation of nature. So far from getting harm there, I fancy I learn something of good; at least, my capacity for enjoyment, which I presume has been given me to be used, is satisfied, and I come away thankful both for the faculty and for the means of gratifying it.'

Another declared that, as far as he was concerned, a broad farce at which he could laugh heartily put him in good humour with himself and all the world for a week afterwards; and in his opinion there was no religion like the religion of good humour. He didn't at all believe in people who thought they were pious when they were only bilious.

To this the Puritan uncle rejoined :

'Your new-fangled notions just make this world everything to you; a place for working, resting, and playing, in turn. Now, I like to follow what the Bible says, and work here while it is day, and look for the wages elsewhere. The harder a man works here the more he will enjoy his rest in heaven.'

'I agree a good deal with uncle,' remarked one who had hitherto been silent, 'and think he is quite right to lay himself out the best he knows how, to procure the greatest amount of enjoyment, whether in this life or a future one. But I like to make the best of what I have got, according to that text he so often reminds us of, which says, "Sufficient for the day." So I try to get as much enjoyment as I can out of this world, and when I get into another, I mean to do the same with that; but not to be always counting on it, and losing a chance here for the sake of a better one there. That would be acting just like nine out of ten miners did when I was in the diggings last season,—always thinking there were better diggings farther on. And the farther off any new diggings were the richer they believed them to be. It would be such a disappointment when one had gone through this world on uncle's plan, to find that there was no more to come. Though I can't help thinking it would only be a fair punishment for re- fusing all the good things Providence has offered us here because we thought they were not good enough and wanted some- thing better.'

Herbert sees here ' the possibility of brethren dwelling together in unity with- out uniformity, where due allowance is made for the natural disposition of each : the attempt to secure uniformity, whether in family, church, or state, being but a

parody on the famous Procrustean bed.
Room for all, and for the development of
all, ought then to be the guiding principle
of every community.'

CHAPTER IX.

BLACK AND WHITE.

HERBERT was much surprised to find the first mentioned of the sons an approver of slavery; the only New Englander he has ever met who held that opinion. But it seems that a keen appreciation of art, and recognition of the rules of taste, are not incompatible with the most eclectic inconsistency in opinions concerning other matters; and the artist's mind is probably attracted as much by a certain picturesqueness in his conception of the institution as by anything else. Taking Herbert into his sleeping-room, which is also his studio, he exhibits a water-colour representation of 'the design of Providence' respecting the negro. It varies from the old pyramidal theory of society in making the broadest basis consist of the whole animal kingdom, instead of the labouring classes of men; and in having a white man instead of a Sovereign for its apex. In the intermediate links he has placed the chimpanzee next to the negro, the whole scale representing a gradual ascent to the highly cultivated European. He has replied to Herbert's argument from the mischievous effects of irresponsible power upon the governing class by saying that all men possess it in respect of other animals, without being the worse for it; and now he points triumphantly to his drawing.

'There's my answer to those who impugn what I believe to be a merciful provision of Providence for the improvement

and protection of an inferior race. Look
at that table of degrees, and point out to
me where, guided by evident resemblance,
you would draw a line which shall have
the animal on one side and the human on
the other.'

The spectator cannot but admit that in
facial aspect the negro resembles the race
below more than that above him, but de-
nies the inference drawn from that resemblance, saying that the question of humanity rests upon psychological even more
than on anatomical qualities, and he suggests that the argument might as well be
carried farther, and a scale drawn of the
various classes of white men having for its
basis those engaged in the lowest and most
degrading occupations, and the most ignorant and depraved classes in town and
country, all in their ordinary condition of
costume, and above these the various
grades up to the highly cultivated and re-

fined gentleman, who should be represented
as clean shaved and in full evening dress.
Where, he asks, in such a scale would ap-
pearances suggest the placing of a line
between those who are fit to rule and those
who require ruling. His friend says that
practically it is impossible to draw a line
between one white man and another, and
that each finds his place in the social scale
according to his opportunities and natural
fitness. That the white is capable of self-
improvement. Not so the negro, who never
will be fit for other than menial offices.

'If that be indeed true,' asks Herbert,
'does it not seem superfluous to supple-
ment nature's irreversible decree by human enactments restricting him to a sphere
he is already incapacitated by his very nature from leaving? You don't legislate
to prevent horses and dogs from assuming
human functions. To do so with the negro
seems to imply distrust of your theory re-

specting his real place in the scale. A
theory it is difficult to imagine people can
really hold who have allowed the two races
to mingle until a very large proportion of
the slaves have almost as much white blood
in them as their owners.' He admits that
this is indeed a crime and a sin, invalid-
ating the claims of the planters to any con-
sideration, but not affecting the abstract
question; and Herbert adds to his notes
the reflection that 'all systems of legislation
which restrain classes to certain spheres of
action are wrong, inasmuch as they imply
either a distrust of the assertion that such
classes are naturally incapable, or else a
conviction that they can improve upon the
order of nature. Our laws about women
come under this category. The just position of all is determinable only by their
natural capacity. If the negro *can* rival
the white, if the woman *can* do the man's
work, they have a natural right to do it.

What is called the man's sphere ceases to be exclusively his. No fear of any real trespass where nature has assigned a real difference. It only shows that man is not in his own peculiar sphere of action when he finds himself encroached on by woman. And not only is the attempt to supersede the inherent laws of things absurd and impious, but it is the wretchedest policy, at once destroying the beautifully adjusted natural relations of the parties, and placing them in a position of antagonism, producing envy, hatred, and strife, towards each other.

' The future remedy of slavery will be found neither in the expulsion of the blacks, nor in their amalgamation with the whites, but in such advance of social knowledge and right feeling as shall permit the two races to be free-dwellers in one State, each preserving its integrity distinct, and fulfilling its own separate function. If the

negro prefer servitude for his inheritance
he will be free to occupy that rank in the
social scale, and there being no compulsion
or jealousy to excite opposition, all parties
will accept their natural position and willingly acknowledge their mutual obligation
and dependence.'

' But how about the blacks having citi-
zen's franchise, and an equal share in the
government? As freemen they would be
entitled to that.'

' And it may be added : and how about
women having it? Alas for the white
man's superior intelligence if it is unre-
cognizable by the black, and alas for that
of the man if he cannot convince the
woman !'

' Then why not universal suffrage in
England ?'

' Ah, why not, except that the people
don't show themselves anxious for it ? Per-

haps they think that they would not govern the country any better. But what
says your father to your slavery principles ? '

'Well, that is a rather sore subject.
But he contents himself with quoting the
golden rule, and says I should not like to
be a slave myself. To which my answer
is that I didn't like being taught or pun-
ished when I was a child, but it was done
nevertheless, and I am not sure that it did
me any harm. I shut up uncle, however,
by telling him that it is an easy thing to
be an Abolitionist in respect of another
person's property. I pity the slaves if
ever they do come to being deprived of
their masters. Whatever our Union is in
practice, in theory it is impossible so long
as the two great sections differ in their
definition of MAN.'

The conversation at supper that even-

ing turned upon negroes and their future
in the States.

'They will follow the Indians and
vanish some day,' said Herbert.

'They'll have votes first,' growled the
Puritan uncle.

'Never!' exclaimed one of the brothers; 'there are reasons physical, and
reasons phrenological, against that.'

'Phrenological!' sneered the uncle.

'Yes, phrenological,' returned the other.
'A white man's brain is divided into cells
and compartments, each of which has its
own particular faculty, and is capable of
any amount of development; but a nigger
has nothing of the kind, no more than a
brute beast. A nigger's brain is one con-
glomerated mass of fat.'

'Don't believe a bit of it,' said the
uncle: 'I hate the very name of that mock
science which makes a man's mind and
soul depend upon the shape or amount of

a bit of flesh. And I don't believe there's an atom of truth in Phrenology.'

'Then the world has been very much mistaken for a vast number of ages,' observed the artist-brother.

'How so, when it's a new invention?' asked the uncle.

'Because there has always been a popular belief in the connection between a man's character and the shape of his head. You yourself acknowledge that much when you call one man "long"-headed, another "thick"-headed, another "bullet"-headed; and when you praise the "splendid forehead" of one, and describe another as having "all his head behind his ears." And the comparative anatomists allow that the moral qualities even of beasts are indicated by the form of their heads.'

'Ah, the general shape, I allow, may have something to do with character, just as one judges by the form and size of a muscle whether it has any power in it.'

' I do not see,' observed Herbert, 'why organization should stop at the eyebrows. I have never heard of any such difference between the inside of a black man's head and a white one's, and am inclined to think that if there be any difference, it is rather in the quality of the brain than in its arrangement. But I do not find it so difficult to suppose that various parts of the brain can be endowed with different faculties, when I find that the various parts of the face are so endowed. One part sees, and another part smells, and another tastes, and another hears; yet if we dissect the membranes or nerves of sensation belonging to those parts, we can discover no difference of form or material to account for the difference of function.'

' Of course if you dissect it, you remove it from its position and destroy its form, which I take to be the principal causes of its different action,' said the artist. 'We are all like steam-engines, more or less, and it is only when the whole is combined and animated by a motive force that each part does its own separate work though the material of each part be exactly the same.'

'You were looking a very long way a-head, it strikes me,' said the father to Herbert, ' when you talked of the negroes dying out. They are increasing now pretty fast. It would be the best thing that could happen to the States, I do believe, but I should like to know how you mean to bring it about.'

'Why the best thing?' asked Herbert.

'Because wherever there are negroes labour is not respectable for the white man, and I take an idle white man to be worse than an industrious nigger.'

'Slavery, then, is more degrading to the whites than to the blacks, and the whites know it?' asked Herbert.

'It is so. Slave or free, the white man won't work with the black.'

'And who are increasing the fastest?'

'Oh, the whites, out and out.'

'And you believe they will never be reconciled to each other?'

'Never.'

'Then the result is as necessary as that of a mathematical problem. The negroes must at last get crowded into a corner by the whites who detest them.'

'Not while slavery lasts. That's the real safeguard of the negro in the States, wicked though it be,' said the father.

'Nigger's best friend,' said the artist.

'Cursed institution,' said the uncle.

'What's to end it?' asked Herbert.

'Buy 'em out,' said the father.

' Give the slaves arms, and let them free themselves,' said the uncle.

' Free the niggers and they are done for,' said the artist.

' Who, which are done for,' asked Herbert, ' negroes or owners ?'

' Both,' shouted all at once.

CHAPTER X.

RED AND BLACK.

ONE of the marvels of San Francisco is its instant transformation at a certain hour each evening from a place of business into a city of hells. The closing of the offices and stores is the signal for the opening of a host of gambling saloons. They are all on the ground floor, well lit, opening on the streets, and so numerous as to excite wonder at night as to where the stores can be, and by day where the saloons are. These are the usual evening resort of all classes. And there are few who do not at least occasionally attempt to win some of the piles of gold and silver that glitter on the tables. Herbert found himself strongly attracted by the thought that it might be possible to cut his labour short by a few fortunate ventures, but he had not done much in one direction or the other when he found himself playing at a table where one of his fellow-passengers was dealing. As he had barely observed the man on board he was rather surprised by his whispering to him in an interval of the game.

'Keep your money in your pocket, and meet me outside at noon to-morrow, and I can do you a good turn.'

'You came here to make money I suppose,' was the greeting when they met next day.

'Certainly.'

'Then take my advice and don't play.'

'Why, is it so difficult to win?' asked Herbert, laughing.

'Difficult! its impossible.'

'But when the chances are so nearly even, surely the interval between the minimum and maximum stake is great enough to allow almost a certainty of winning.'

'Not a bit of it,' was the answer, 'no matter how you arrange your stakes, in the long run its just the same as if they were all of one size; you'll win as many as you lose, and have the per centage of the bank against you.'

'Then all those systems and calculations which I see people following are a delusion?'

'Entirely so. They are merely playing against a certain event which is bound, in the long run, to happen just once in the time it takes for them to win as much as they lose when the event happens, so that they can make nothing by it.'

'But surely some events are far rarer than others and may be considered impossible,' observed Herbert.

'Nothing is impossible to the cards, because the events don't depend on each other,' was the answer; and he continued,

'This dollar has only two sides. Suppose I toss it up and you guess wrong, does that make you any more likely to guess right next time? certainly not; I've seen men guess wrong more than twenty times together. Besides, if you play only against a very rare event your winnings will be proportionably small; and consequently, in order to double your capital, you must play so long as to give the event a good chance of happening. Supposing you play against losing ten times running, you can tell exactly how often you will do so by reckoning how much your stake becomes if left on to win ten times running. One piece doubling up ten times becomes a thousand and twenty-four, therefore just once in that number of coups you must lose or win ten times running; and you must play that number of coups to win as much as you lose when it comes. The game can't be played without risking to lose as much as you can win, and the best way of doing that is to put down the whole sum at once. You have just as good a chance of doubling it as by any way of dividing it into small stakes, and you don't expose it to being dribbled away in per centages to the bank. But if you are wise you won't touch the thing at all. I noticed you in the Killooney, and though we never spoke that I recollect, I took a liking to you, and I don't mind telling you that you are too good for the business. If you have won keep what you have got,

and if you have lost put up with it. No
gambler is ever the richer for winning,
and many a good man becomes a scoundrel
through it.'

'Two or three further conversations
with my professional friend,' writes Herbert in his notes, 'and a careful analysis
of the chances in figures, convince me that
he is right as to the impossibility of winning by systematic play. Any system
may win for a time, but all must lose
eventually. In a game of pure chance
luck is everything: and in the long-run
that must equalize itself. In the mean
time the bank is gaining a certain steady
profit, and the maximum stake is placed
so low as to prevent any extraordinary
event from inflicting a serious loss upon
it. I have discovered that I am no
gambler, since I do not care to play unless
I think I have a certainty of winning. I
can quite understand any one being in-

terested in constructing various systems to play by until the discovery comes that none are infallible. I have made several, and examined many more, each of which at first seemed as if they must win for ever; but, fortunately, instead of testing them by actual experience, I showed them to my professional friend, who soon demonstrated their weak point. He says that when I thoroughly understand the chances I shall leave off figuring. He says the very fact of a chance being even makes it impossible to beat it, otherwise it wouldn't be even. It is a great pity. It would be such an easy way of making a fortune if one could sit down for a few hours a-day, and, without risk or labour, make a certain sum. I don't see why there should be such a prejudice against "gambling" in itself. Every undertaking in life is a venture, more or less doubtful.

All these merchants here are liable to fail. Every profession, marriage itself, is a lottery, in which the future happiness of a life depends on an experiment that cannot be undone. This Californian expedition of mine is nothing less. Perhaps the necessity of labour and judgment are redeeming points in all but mere chance speculations. Probably the real evil of gambling consists in its looking only to the end or reward, and affording no employment for the higher faculties in the pursuit. It is impossible to fancy any artist attaining a high degree of inspiration who thinks solely of the money he is to get for his work. I see how it is with me. In this, as in all my other engrossments, I have been seeking for the Absolute. It seems to me a species of Atheism to say that there is no infallible system, even for playing Monté.

'The remark that "in the long-run nothing is impossible because the events do
not depend on each other," seems capable
of being applied to a very different line
of thought. If in the long-run of events
all things can happen, there can be no
demonstration of a special providence,
neither can a man who believes in the
absence of a controlling Will or Character,
have any reason for objecting to any system of religion on the score of its improbability. However great may be the
chances against an event, those chances
are only against its occurring at any given
moment. If the opportunity be repeated
exactly as often as there are chances
against the event, it is an even chance
that it occurs once in that number of times.
If oftener, the chances are actually in favour of its happening. It is an even
chance every time whether red or black

wins; yet I am told that one has been known to win thirty times together. The odds against such a series are over a thousand millions to one; but in that number of attempts it becomes an even chance that it occurs. And, inasmuch as the past and future are entirely independent of each other, the most improbable event may show itself directly the game begins, and may be repeated many times in rapid succession. Moreover, an event is brought no nearer to happening after the game has gone on for an indefinite time without its coming. It does not become more likely after, or less likely before, many hands have been dealt. Under the government of chance, therefore, the most violently improbable event not only may, but must, sooner or later occur. But the term improbable cannot be properly applied to that which is inevitable. It must be ex-

punged from the vocabulary of chance, or
restricted to signify only *rare*, and that
only in proportion to other events which
are less so.   There is no "improbability"
in infinity.   If then the fortuitous con-
course of atoms, unguided by any instinct,
ungoverned by any law of uniformity, has
resulted in millions of systems and worlds
compounded in varying proportions and
existing under varying conditions, there
must be as many sets of circumstances for
these worlds to exist in, as there are worlds:
and one of these combinations may form
what is called the "Christian scheme."   Or,
if there be but one world, and an indefinite
number of possible schemes, some one of
these must have been hit on for that world
in spite of the number of chances against
it, and that one might be the Christian
scheme.   Its being violently improbable
has been shown to be no reason against it,
since, some one being inevitable, all had

a chance. The Atheist, or believer in chance, therefore, has no argument against Christianity, or any other form of religion, on the ground of *a priori* improbability. He may, consistently with his creed, be a believer, if not a devout one, in the system that comprises the Fall and the Incarnation, Salvation and Damnation. For the believer in a God of unvarying and consistent character, whose visible creation bears the impress of his mind, it is different. Such an one must argue from what is good in a human sense to what is good in a divine sense. Seeing that power, and justice, and tenderness, and purity are among the highest attributes of the most perfect human nature, he necessarily infers that they exist in the greatest perfection in the divine nature. He is therefore unable to recognize as God one who is feeble and baffled, unjust, implacable, and the sustainer of the perpetual pollution of a hell: for all these attributes are indubitably indicated by the details of the orthodox faith. The believer in One God and Father of all, cannot be a believer in the Christianity of the churches. The Atheist, or believer in blind chance, alone can consistently be a 'good Christian;' alone can receive as a grave verity the sublime irony of the Athanasian Creed. I think it is Babbage who has applied the doctrine of chances to the support of the Christian faith. I wonder whether his argument and conclusions at all coincide with mine.'

BOOK IV.

'Sometimes his religion seemed to me
Self-taught, as of a dreamer in the woods,
Who to the model of his own pure heart
Shaped his belief as grace divine inspired,
Or human reason dictated with awe.'

WORDSWORTH's 'Excursion.'

CHAPTER I.

A MINING SETTLEMENT.

Rumours are reaching California that
a great rival to her has started up in the
far South:—that in Australia have been
found gold-fields equal to hers. So flatter-
ing are the accounts, both of the richness
of the mines and of the condition of society
in them, it being said to consist not of men
only, but of whole families, that Herbert is
strongly tempted thither. The experience
he has gained will be most valuable there,
and he feels a yearning to be among his
own countrymen again. He determines,

however, to try one more winter in the
Sierra Nevada, in company with an English doctor, with whom he has fraternized,
who has lived long in South America, and
has for the last year been mining in California.

Herbert and his new companion 'make
tracks' from the Bay straight for a far
distant settlement, near the source of the
Yuba.   It is called Downieville, and is
surrounded by diggings of extraordinary
richness.   Lying at the bottom, as it were,
of a tremendous well, so steep and lofty
are the mountains which immediately close
it in, it is difficult of access even on foot.
American energy and ingenuity however
contrive to supply a considerable population with food.   By lashing trees to their
waggons, and making their oxen pull back
up the hill in order to retard their downward progress, the feat of carriage is safely
performed.   Certainly it is a rich spot,—

yielding its gold in no tiny specks, but in beautiful large lumps. But the ground is all occupied, and the two new comers can only look enviously on as they walk among the claims and see in one hole a couple of sailors picking out eight or ten pounds weight a day, and in another men not overstating their gains at a hundred dollars for every hour they choose to work.

Herbert and the doctor at once commence a search among the neighbouring ravines for similar spots. While thus engaged Herbert does not omit to make a few notes illustrative of the state of society in the settlement. People generally are too well off to steal; they all possess something of their own, and can therefore respect the property of others. Violence is more common, arising out of quarrels over drink and gambling. One day, however, a man is taken before the Justice for stealing sundry pairs of boots. He is found guilty, and adjudged to restore the stolen property, and by way of fine, to ' treat all hands.'

Whereupon the officers of the court, accompanied by his Worship and the whole crowd present, adjourn to the nearest tavern (which by a singular coincidence happens to belong to the Justice in question), and, together with the culprit, drink at his expense. He gets so laughed at that he probably will never steal again, few things being harder to bear than ridicule. Such is the moral that circulates with the liquor through the jovial assemblage. Indeed they enjoy the joke so much, and are so desirous of exhibiting their detestation of thieving, that they stop and drink several times on the same score. The Justice himself becomes somewhat excited ; so much so, that it does not occur to him that he may be inflicting a far heavier fine than the prisoner can pay. When at last the score is reckoned up and payment required, not only is the money not forthcoming, but the man also is missing, having taken advantage of the general engrossment to slip out, and pack up his wardrobe, and make the best of his start to escape over the hills and far away! Unfortunate Justice, who better than thyself can now tell how hard to bear is ridicule? to say nothing of the fine which thou hast inflicted upon—thine own pocket!

Perhaps it would be well if judges were more frequently to taste the effects of their own sentences. The comedy over, but a short interval passes before the curtain rises for a tragedy.

There is a party of Mexicans in Downieville, one of whom, a woman, receives some bitter provocation from an American. In her fury she stabs him, so that he dies. So great was the provocation that some admit that had the murder been committed by an American it would have merited

little reprobation. But the Mexicans are
in bad odour throughout the country. And
the friends of the dead man are furious,
and work up the rest until it is determined
to hang her. Herbert begs the Justice to
use his influence to save her. 'It would
cost him his place,' he says.

'But you know perfectly well that they
are going to hang her for being a Mexican.'

'May be, but I advise you not to say
that outside.'

'At any rate you can get it postponed
until the people cool down?'

'Can't be done. They keep from
work, and guard her day and night, and
there will be hardly a sober man in the
place until it is over.'

Herbert talks to a few others, among
them to a candidate who happens to be
present canvassing for his election to the
legislature. They admit the justice of his

remonstrances, but remind him that in the United States everything is decided by the majority, and the majority can do no wrong. He finds it difficult to convince them that justice is altogether independent of majorities; that might does not make right, and so forth.

' May be, but here the majority govern. You have only got to get them to think with you.'

Entering into a general conversation with the crowd in a saloon, he ventures to urge its postponement for a week, that justice might be done in cool blood: otherwise it will be mere revenge, of which they may be ashamed when too late. Being recognized as a ' Britisher ' his interference rather enrages them than otherwise. And his attempt ends in his learning that the American populace, in spite of their pretensions, have no more real conception of true liberty than the members of an English trades' union. They cannot imagine it possible for a majority of the people to act tyrannically. To make it tyranny, they think it must be the act of one or a few.

He was a consistent American therefore who said to Herbert in Central America on seeing a priest walking in the streets in his canonicals;—

'There, Sir, he couldn't do that in New York. Ours is a free country, and the majority won't allow it.'

'A free country, indeed!' was the rejoinder; 'where a man can't wear what clothes he pleases.'

The appointed time arrives. The poor Mexican is brought to the place of execution. Her dark eyes flash round exultingly on the crowd as she declares in broken English, that she would do the same again to any man who should treat her in the same way.

Taking her long black hair in her hands, she holds it up carefully at arm's length so as to allow the rope to be adjusted beneath it, and then allows it to hang its whole length downwards, and so dies without an effort.

CHAPTER II.

HIGHER STILL AND HIGHER.

MEANWHILE Herbert and his companion are laboriously arriving at the conviction that all the good ground in that vicinity is occupied. The doctor has proved a capital fellow for the kind of life, working like a horse when there is anything to be done, and smoking like a factory chimney at all other seasons. He does a little doctoring too; and having due appreciation of the superiority of his own British qualifications over those of all Americans whatever, does not fail to demand ample remuneration for the exercise of his skill. To patients who remonstrate with him on the exorbitance of his charge, he loves to reply, 'Think what my medical education cost; that has to be paid for!' which from one canny Scotchman elicits the retort, 'Certainly, doctor, that's only fair; but not all at once.'

Disappointed in the diggings, and little pleased with the people, they determine to strike out into a new country. Discoveries of amazing richness are reported, some two hundred miles away, near the boundaries of Oregon, and but few persons have as yet reached the spot. The journey thither is a formidable one; that is, it would be to any but gold-hunters. But this pursuit seems to endow its devotees with a power of despising dangers and subduing difficulties, altogether unimaginable to ordinary stay-at-home mortals; physical difficulties, at least: as for moral ones, people at home are probably quite as ready to surmount any such that may lie in the way of their making money. A fixed idea is apt to blind its possessor to everything except itself. Not without method, however, do the two adventurers go about their purpose. There are no maps, but they know the general conformation of the mountain ranges; that the rivers all run in parallel lines from the main range of the Sierra Nevada, which lies in a tolerably straight course between north and south, projecting at right angles and equal intervals long lines of hills, between which run the rivers towards the western ocean. The place of their destination is high up on the northernmost of these streams, within the Californian territory. Starting therefore from their present position, their journey must be parallel to the main mountain-range, but right across the great ridges and their intervening rivers. How rugged and steep these ridges may be, or how rapid and deep the rivers, or how many and fierce the Indian tribes by the way, they know not. But the ridges they will surmount. The precipices they will scale or go round. The rivers they will ford or swim; and the Indians they will avoid, parley with, or, if need be, fight. So, with two stout horses carrying a month's supply of provisions, consisting mainly of dried meat, flour, rice, and such things as are most compact and lightest, packed on their saddles, Herbert and the doctor, armed with knives and pistols, climb the steep hill at the back of Downieville while the morning is still dark. For Downieville is a dangerous place for men to be seen leaving; and those suspected of having money are sometimes followed and attacked.

The rising sun greets them while breathing their horses on the hill-top after an ascent of some four thousand feet. Here the hills appear broken into a confused collection of ridges in which no regular plan is apparent, and making it impossible long together to follow any set direction. Looking down upon them are two mountains that, from their height and peculiar form, will serve as landmarks through many a long day's journey. One is called the Saddle Mountain, from the shape of its summit, and the other 'Los Dedos,' the fingers, from its resemblance to a hand pointing upwards. There is no forest here to impede their view or their progress. All is rough broken rock, as bare as on the day when it first emerged from the abyss, with the exception of a few stunted shrubs. There is no trail of white man or red. Their destination lies due north; and the sun rising on the right hand alone indicates their course.

No sooner up than down again. Each leading his horse, they cross the ridge and commence a rapid descent.   At the bottom, at the same depth as that from which they had already started that morning, is a stream, which their horses are able to ford. They then commence climbing the most promising parts of the mountain before them.   In places it is very steep, so that they can only get their horses up by carrying their picket-ropes forwards, planting themselves behind jutting rocks, and fairly hauling them up.   Much of the ground is covered with loose angular rocks, which turn over when stepped upon; and sometimes the brush is so thick as to be almost impenetrable.   Herbert, in his letter home, describes this part of their route to be like passing over the tops of houses, climbing down the sides, crossing the streets, and climbing up the opposite side.

The first evening they come upon a charming little hollow in the summit of a mountain, circled round the edges with a

bank of snow, and richly carpeted with
grass in the centre, and flowers growing at
the very edge of the snow.   Here they
bivouack under some dry pines, to one of
which they set fire, first ascertaining that
they all incline from them.   The fire soon
spreads from one to the other; and during
the night they are guarded from the presence of obnoxious Grislys by nine tall
columns of flame.   In the morning, however, there is ice all around them.   Reaching one of the southern branches of the
Feather river, they encamp in a fine valley,
well grassed and somewhat too well watered,
for the doctor gets a severe attack of fever
and ague.   This necessitates a pause, and
while the doctor is alternately burning and
shivering, Herbert prospects the country
round, but finds nothing more exchange-
able than granite.   While here the hopes
they have built upon the new diggings
meet with a sudden dash; for they fall in

with men coming from the very spot for which they are bound, who report that the new gold-field is so limited in extent that a thousand men have hunted through the whole neighbourhood and found nothing, and that the road is, if possible, worse than that which they have already passed over. They decide, therefore, to go no farther in that direction, but to follow up the stream on which they are, to its source, prospecting as they go; and then, if nothing be found to induce them to stay, to mount the main range of the Sierra Nevada, and travel along the ridge back to the Yuba, hoping thus to avoid the break-neck country already traversed. They are able to purchase fresh beef of the men they have met. This, cut into strips and dried in the sun, furnishes provision for some time. A week sees the doctor able to travel again. Their steeds also are thoroughly renovated, and they start up the stream. Though disappointed in the immediate object of their expedition, they are by no means depressed; for is not the whole mountain-range before them, in which it is generally supposed that the gold has its origin? There is certainly some reason for the belief, for experience has already shown that the lumps in which gold is found are larger and larger the farther up in the hills it is sought for; and it is almost an article of faith with miners as well, writes Herbert, as with seekers for truth, that if they only go far enough they will find the solid parent mass from which, with hammer and chisel, they can cut off as much as they desire.

Without quite entertaining such an idea, it is little wonder that the hopes of the two travellers were raised on reaching a mountain of quartz, so white and massive as to appear like snow at a little distance; for gold is always found associated with quartz. It forms the matrix in which the precious metal was originally formed,—the mould in which it was cast.

Before commencing any search for gold, the first thing to be found is grass and water. A small sheltered hollow, studded with immense masses of milk-white rock, affords all that is needed in these respects; and a careful search is commenced in the mountain-side, and ravines, and all places in which gold ordinarily lodges. It proves however a barren mountain, too isolated in its white purity to produce even the divine metal, and leading Herbert to suspect that, even in the mineral system, duality is necessary to fruitfulness; all the quartz in which he has found gold containing also iron in the form of pyrites, and being often exquisitely coloured by it. These damp, grassy hollows prove unwholesome sleeping places. Fever and ague again make their appearance; and this

time Herbert is the victim. During a
week's inactivity the magic bark of Peru
accomplishes its work, and the travellers
set themselves towards the last great rise
of the Sierra Nevada. Their stock of provisions is so far diminished that they can
both ride, whenever the country admits of
riding; and they begin somewhat anxiously
to think that it will be well to look out for
a replenishment, in the shape of some
venison. Once on the top of the mountain,
a week's journey ought to take them back
into a more settled district. The idea of
retracing their steps is not for a moment
entertained; such is the invincible charm
of mystery and adventure. Indeed Herbert
is amused by noting of himself how the
same peculiarity of disposition which impels him to uncontrolled excursiveness of
thought, seems to govern also his actual
career. 'Character,' says Emerson, 'is
destiny.' No doubt, when once formed.

But how about the destiny that precedes and determines the character? What Herbert specially marks in his own case is the precise unison between the two parts of his nature—the physical and the mental. He fancies he discerns in this some proof that what is called man's higher or spiritual nature, is but a result of his physical organism; or, at least, that the two are so closely connected and interdependent that their separate existence is by no means imaginable to us. As the summer has seen him plunging into the remotest reaches of thought, in search of absolute and unattainable truth, with no guide or safeguard but his own perceptions,—so the fall of the year finds him wandering in the wildest and most terrible wilderness of the New World; leaving the places of certain, though limited, remuneration, in search of the uncertain and unlimited: with no knowledge of the country, beyond a vague theory of its formation, and no guide or compass beyond the sun and stars. 'For once,' he thinks, 'I am but doing as I have been taught. For what else do they who reject the certain though limited pleasures of this life, for the uncertain and unlimited ones of another?'

CHAPTER III.

A DESCENT.

IT is near sun-down when the wanderers reach the summit of the mountain. They find themselves in a large basin, crowded with vegetation, groves of trees with thick underwood, and plenty of grass and water, and abundant tracks of deer and other animals. No signs of Indians have been seen for so long that they deem themselves secure from molestation from that quarter, and are therefore unconcerned about the tremendous blaze made by some dozen dry pines to which their fire extends. Next morning, while riding slowly across the basin, a herd of deer appear feeding under the trees some two hundred yards off. Herbert gives his rein to the doctor, cautioning him not to move, and, pistol in hand, (for they had deemed rifles too cumbrous in the rough country they expected to traverse), advanced stealthily from tree to tree until within shot. He had made his selection and was in the act of taking aim, when a shout from the doctor called his attention to two Indians who were approaching in a menacing attitude from another direction. The startled deer at once take themselves off, and he hastens towards the doctor and the horses to be in readiness for flight or action. Seeing the two white men quietly awaiting them, the Indians, who were armed with bows and spears, paused about fifty paces distant, and made signs to Herbert, who was still on foot, to advance and meet one of

them half way, the doctor and the other
Indian remaining where they were ; a
natural precaution against treachery. So
Herbert went forward to hold a colloquy
with the Indian. Knowing that a con-
fident bearing would be interpreted as a
conviction of certain superiority, he walks
straight up to the savage, smiles at him,
and shakes hands, not doubting that he
has heard that such is the custom of the
whites, and asks if he is hungry. Was
there ever a red-skin that was not hungry near the hour of sun-rise ? Come
along and have something to eat then.
So the two Indians seeing it is peace,
which is evidently a great relief to their
minds, as it no doubt is to the rest of
the party, come up to the doctor, and fall
to upon some bread and boiled beans,
and take a pull at the doctor's pipe, and
through excess of courtesy or timidity,
even pretend that they like it. They

have some words in common with the other tribes, and so are tolerably intelligible to Herbert. It appears that last night's fire attracted their attention and astonishment, and being in the midst of their favourite hunting-ground, had excited the anger of the whole tribe. Suspecting the presence of a hostile tribe, they had sent out small parties in different directions to reconnoitre, agreeing to meet at the place of the fire. Their rancheria was on the western side of the mountain, and they advise the intruders to cross over and descend into the valley on the other side before the rest of the tribe come up. Herbert intimates that they have come there with no desire to frighten away the game, but merely to travel along the ridge towards the white men's settlements.

The manifest anxiety of the Indians to get rid of them appears too real to be assumed, and they ascribe it to a desire to prevent a collision with the rest of the tribe, the issue of which their ignorance of the white man's resources renders doubtful. They therefore signify to the Indians their intention of quitting the mountain, and, desirous of concealing their exact route, caution them not to follow them.

The two Indians remain rooted to the spot until the horsemen are hidden behind a dense thicket. Certain that they can no longer be observed, Herbert and the doctor then change their course, and proceed along the edge of the mountain until they can obtain a view of the country beyond. Clear of the trees, they behold a vast plain stretching out from the base of the range and extending on each side farther than the eye can reach; a sea of grass it seems at that height, unbroken by tree or rock. If obliged to descend, they can make good travelling in the valley by keeping near the foot of the hills. But hoping to elude

the Indians, they continue along just below the brow for some distance, intending
to return and pursue their way along the
top when out of their immediate territory.

They are thus but a short way down
the hill-side when they perceive that they
are being watched from above. Vain hope,
to outwit the wild man on his own ground.
No doubt it is the same pair with whom they
have already spoken, and who have since
invisibly dogged every step of their way.
But these have been joined by two others.
Without betraying that they have discovered the Indians, Herbert and the
doctor change their course for a more
downward one, until hidden in an almost
impenetrable thicket of brushwood. Here
they pause and hold counsel. On the
rough and tangled ridge they are evidently
at the mercy of the savages, for there the
speed of their horses can avail them nothing. While in the plain the greater dis-

tance will be compensated by greater ease in travelling ; and if attacked, they will at least be able to run away. So the resolve is taken to descend into the vast valley below, and follow the base of the mountain until they judge themselves opposite the head of the Yuba, and then remount the ridge and follow the stream down to the settlements.

The first thing to be done, therefore, is to reach the bottom. At present the descent is gradual enough, but it is impossible to say what precipices await them lower down. Already much care is necessary in leading their horses among the sharp rocks, and thorny bushes, and fallen trees, that encumber the mountain-side, for should one of them become lamed their predicament is indeed an awkward one. Indeed it is beginning to look bad enough now, for the spur of the mountain by which they are descending, instead of

sloping gradually into the valley, ends abruptly in a hideous precipice while they
are scarcely half way down. From the
brink of the cliff they can see another spur
which promises a safe descent if they can
reach it. To do this it is necessary to re-
trace their path for a little way, and then
clamber along the mountain-side for about
a quarter of a mile. With much toil about
half this distance is accomplished, when
farther progress is arrested by the ravine
that divides the two spurs. Down this
rushes a torrent, making vast noise and
splash as it leaps over the perpendicular
rock far overhead, and dashes down among
a huge tangled mass of trees fallen and
stripped, and inextricably knotted together
with the thorny growth of many seasons,
the whole forming an impenetrable barrier.
On the farther side the rock continues its
perpendicular front, but along the base of
it runs a narrow ledge which seemed to

open out after a little into easier ground. By climbing over the fallen trees they get on this ledge and find the path passable enough if they can only get their horses over to it. Just below their standing-ground the ravine is crossed by the trunk of a pine some three feet in diameter, the root of which rests on the ledge opposite, and the end slopes down to their own side, reaching it about ten yards below them. Herbert walks back over this log after exploring the path. The bark is all off, and the surface is sound, and white, and slippery, but it yields beneath his tread as if rotten inside. If they can only get the horses over they can get on well enough, and this log is the only bridge. With the spade and pick-axe carried for mining, he tests the trunk and finds the wood sufficiently soft for working. The doctor joins him, and in about an hour a broad strip of the outer surface is removed, and the brown

rotten interior partially scooped out or
trodden down, so as to form a trough reaching right across the gulf. The noise of
the torrent has probably concealed the
sound of their working from the savages
who are no doubt accumulating above
them. After some trouble one of the
horses is induced to step upon the log,
Herbert going first leading him by the
rein, and the doctor steadying him by
holding the tail. Their united weight
tries the strength of the bridge rather se-
verely, but the thin outer shell being of a
tubular form and therefore not likely to
break, only suggests to Herbert a joke
about their being in 'many straits' together, which he propounds for the doctor's encouragement. Approaching the
centre the vibrations increase, and the
chasm below assumes an exceedingly uncomfortable aspect. It is impossible to
turn back, and there is nowhere to go to

if they could. So, pausing a moment, Herbert uncoils the rope from the animal's neck and goes forward with it to the end, and then draws the poor horse towards him. Seeing all go well the doctor steps back, and the log, relieved of the weight of the two men, proves equal to its work; the two horses are safely landed on the desired ledge, which soon opens upon a gradually sloping spur, affording an easy descent into the valley. Here the horses are allowed to fill themselves with rich, sweet grass, while their riders, less fortunate, for they have sacrificed the principal portion of their day's allowance in order to propitiate the Indians, content themselves with a few mouthfuls of bread and meat, and resolve to ride some twenty miles farther before stopping for the night, so as to be quite clear of the tribe in the mountain. They can both ride now, for the horses have little else to carry. The delays caused by the sickness, first of one, and then of the other, have made sad havoc with the stock of provisions; and now that they have left the mountain there is not the same chance of meeting with deer, or getting within pistol-shot of them. On camping for the night they take stock of their provisions, and are dismayed to find how small the quantity has become. By limiting their daily ration to about six ounces apiece, they will hold out for eight or ten days. Before going to sleep they cook enough to last two days, making this time a very small fire indeed. The doctor gets into a state of consternation on finding how low his supply of tobacco has got, and the discovery is also made that in coming through the brush the package containing ammunition has been torn open, and nearly all the powder has run out. Half a dozen charges may remain, certainly not more.

CHAPTER IV.

THE OTHER SIDE.

NOTHING occurs to interrupt the night's rest; and the rising sun reveals a large lake, reaching almost to the foot of the hills, and melting away in the distance. Pursuing their onward course, they make a detour towards the lake; for they have fish-hooks and lines, and a piece of water of that size cannot be without fish. The ground over which they are riding is covered with long grass, and to their surprise, they go two or three miles out into the plain without reaching the water. At

some distance ahead it seems to bend towards the hills again; so they resume their
course, in order to get round its extremity.
Reaching the foot of the hills, they ascend
a little way, so as to overlook the valley.
The lake is there sure enough, covered
with a thin blue mist, and far beyond a
line of hills is dimly visible above it.   By
night they have gone some forty miles, but
still without being able to get close to the
lake.   Herbert assuages his hunger as they
ride along by chewing the ears of the tall
grass; and the doctor, in order to make the
remnant of his tobacco last as long as possible, sucks at his empty pipe.

They make no fire that night, but sup
upon a small cake of flour which had been
baked over-night; and for breakfast they
warm up a small quantity of beans.   The
horses, however, feed gloriously.   Two or
three hours on their backs makes their
riders feel as if they had not breakfasted

at all; and it is determined to make an
early noon, and try the effect of boiling a
small quantity of grass. They have never
heard of anybody eating grass since the
days of Nebuchadnezzar; but it seems to
have agreed with him: why should it not
agree with them? What is all grain but a
species of grass, with merely altered proportions of ear and stalk? And really,
when boiled and the water is poured off, it
looks much like spinach, and with a little
salt, is not so very insipid to the taste.
The discovery puts them in good spirits;
but a few hours' riding reminds them that
even horses cannot with impunity change
to a grass diet, and long before supper-time
arrives, both Herbert and the doctor are
forced to the conclusion that the experiment is a decided failure. They determine, however, to try it again after a day
or two, with the addition of oak leaves, or
bark, to make it more astringent. The

next day, after riding a few miles, they perceive a smoke rising from among the trees. There are trails in the grass, showing the neighbourhood of some tribe; and, too hungry to hesitate, they ride up in hope of finding some Indians, and getting fish from them. But they find the fire abandoned, and no signs to indicate what has been cooked by it.

The next day a couple of shots are thrown away after some deer, there being no cover to allow a near approach. Towards sunset, when selecting a spot for camping, a grouse or 'prairie hen' gets up in front of Herbert. Drawing his pistol from the holster, he fires at it. The bird flies about a hundred yards and drops head foremost, evidently dead. Doctor shouts joyously in anticipation of his supper, and rides to pick it up. There is a good deal of brushwood about, and they hunt for it until quite dark, and at length have to lie down with nothing more than their ordinary morsel—'five teaspoonsful of boiled beans each.' At dawn the search is renewed, but with no better success. They are so hungry that the disappointment is felt most bitterly.

The valley now begins to get narrowed by the closing in of the farther range of hills. All appearance of the great lake has vanished, and they ride on in doubt as to whether it was really a lake or only a mirage that had deceived them. It is about ten o'clock when something appears, moving in the distance before them. Coming nearer, it proves to be a man on horseback, —a solitary horseman, who does not shun them. It must be a white man, and they are getting *somewhere* at last.

No ; it is an Indian, with a bow in his hand, a splendid-looking fellow, who rides up close without hesitation, and commences to chat in a very unintelligible dialect.

He is clad in a deer-skin, thrown with careless elegance over his shoulders. His rein
is a strip of the same material. Without
any saddle, he sits his horse in easy and
graceful manner, and now and then gallops
off a little way in search of game; occasionally drawing up his arrow nearly to the
head, as if to keep his arm in practice.

The native bow of California is a very
handy one for use on horse-back, being
only some thirty inches long; the wood of
the country not affording length for the
ordinary long bow.

In this manner he guides them through
a difficult swamp to his rancheria. Here,
dwelling in bush huts, they find a small
family of Indians, consisting of a couple,
—old, almost blind, and wrinkled as
baboons,—and three fine young men, with
their wives and children. The men come
out boldly, while the women and children
peer curiously through the bushes at the

strangers. The old man examines the blankets and clothes, and takes especial pleasure in stroking the panther-skin covers of Herbert's holsters, with which he appears greatly impressed; turning away at last with a broad, satisfied grin of delight upon his face, as if indicating that having seen a white man he can now depart in peace. The usual present of fish-hooks and string is made, the Indians showing their comprehension of their use by immediately putting them into their own mouths, and making as if they had hooked themselves.

The whole family are so friendly that the two wanderers determine to rest with them, and recruit themselves, provided they can get some food from them. On signifying their need, the Indians produce some swamp-roots from a heap in one of the huts, intimating that when roasted they are very good. Remembering their recent experience, Herbert and the doctor examine

and taste them somewhat distrustfully, and
at length determine to cook them. There
is no fire in the camp, so they begin to
collect some sticks, which the Indians no
sooner see than they despatch two of the
children, who run towards the hill, and
soon return with dry brushwood, which
they lay before their guests, and with the
rest of the family stand round to watch
their proceedings, evidently anticipating a
vast difficulty in lighting the requisite fire.
Making a small pile of broken twigs, and
placing some dry leaves beneath, Herbert
draws forth a small tin box, and takes out
a match. At this point the interest becomes intense. Drawing the match sharply
over the rough side of the box, a slight report is heard, and the match appears in a
blaze, which being applied to the dry leaves,
the fire is kindled. The excitement now
is general. The children caper about and
the men run to the huts, and report to the

old couple and the women the wonderful
ease with which the white men have made
fire. The roasted roots are bitter, but by
no means bad. On asking for something
more substantial, the Indians consult together, and intimate that by the time the
sun gets low they hope to procure something else. Two of them take their bows
and arrows, and are absent all the after-
noon, during which the doctor dresses the
hand of the third man, which is much
swollen by a large thorn being deeply
buried in it. The production of a pocket-
case of surgical instruments is the signal
for much curiosity, and the whole tribe
manifests a degree of awe at the prowess of
the mighty medicine-man of the pale faces,
as he inspects the wound, solemnly com-
mands the patient to lie down and look the
other way, and directs Herbert to hold the
arm still while he makes an incision with
a lancet, and then with a minute pair of

tweezers, draws forth the offending thorn, and exhibits it to the admiring spectators. The Indian bears the pain of the operation, which must have been considerable, with fortitude, but cannot help wincing under the terrible squeeze with which the doctor expels the last drop of blood and matter that exudes from the wound. Rarely does man look happier than the poor patient as he sits bathing his hand in cold water until all pain is gone, assured that now he will soon be quite well, and able to join his brothers in the chase. The whole party share in his joy, running forward to meet and tell the hunters, as they return with their spoil, consisting of a number of field-mice, and a couple of squirrels, which they place at their guests' disposal. Somewhat to the surprise of the Indians, they take only the squirrels. The matches are again in requisition; this time the entire family crowding round to witness the magic process of ignition. The whole of the game is then roasted in the embers, and the party feast merrily together. Next morning the travellers take leave of the kind-hearted savages with mutual regret, conferring on them unbounded wealth by giving them a small stock of matches, having shown them how to ignite them on a flat stone, and explained that they must be kept dry.

Two of the Indians run before them on the trail along the valley, every now and then discharging an arrow at some small bird, which, though they shoot with marvellous precision, generally contrives to get out of the way before the arrow reaches it, as if too well acquainted with the missile to care to wait for it. Presently they approach a small pool surrounded by reeds. Motioning to the riders to keep back, the Indians creep through the rushes to the edge, and letting fly at the same moment, one of

them shoots a duck through the body, and
the other shoots one through the head.
These they present to their white friends,
and before parting with them endeavour to
dissuade them from continuing their present course, and energetically point over
the hills to the west. Not comprehending their object, and judging that they
must go yet farther before they reach
that part of the mountain which is opposite to the settlements, Herbert and the
doctor continue along the valley. The
two Indians, on seeing this, insist on
accompanying them, still pointing to the
hills on the right. At length, finding all
their remonstrances vain, they pause, and
with looks of deep dejection and sorrow
stand watching them until out of sight.

CHAPTER V.

LOST.

ON waking next morning the travellers are surprised to find a strange horse and mule feeding beside their own. The doctor thinks that the mule, being the fattest, may afford them a supply of meat, but is met by the objection that their owners are probably not far off and will resent any such appropriation. Presently two Indians are seen approaching to take the animals. They betray unbounded astonishment at the sight of the white men. With some trouble they are induced to come near, and after receiving a small present they return with their animals. Having, as they hope, propitiated the tribe through these two emissaries, Herbert and the doctor soon follow in the same direction. They have gone about two miles when they are met by some forty Indians, the largest and fiercest-looking savages they have yet seen, all devoid of clothing, and armed with bows and spears. They at once close round the travellers and examine them, and everything they have, making signs that they want them. A gift of fish-hooks and string seems only to whet their appetite.

Not liking the looks of the savages, who keep increasing in number, the two horsemen trot on at a smart pace, accompanied by the whole troop; some seizing their bridles, and all whooping and leaping over the rocks and bushes as they rush along in

full career, until they come in sight of the
rancheria. Then they set up a yell, which
is responded to by the rest of the tribe,
who are awaiting their return. They
evidently consider Herbert and the doctor
as captives conducted in triumph to their
village. There is still a space of two or
three hundred yards between the two
bodies when this occurs to Herbert. They
may be acting only as a guard of honour
to the strangers, but the appearance of
their escort is by no means prepossessing.
So Herbert desires the two Indians who
are running at his horse's head to fall back.
They only grasp the bridle more tightly,
and he calls out to the doctor, who is close
behind him, to put spurs to his horse and
get clear of their present escort before
they can effect a junction with the party
in front. Doctor says,

'All right! but which way?'

'Straight ahead! through the village and along the valley, for they will soon catch us if we turn into the hills!'

Then suddenly snatching his bridle out of the Indians' hands, Herbert plunges his spurs into his horse's sides, leaps clear of them, and gallops on. The doctor does the same, and presently the whole troop is left behind, with the exception of two, who still run on before at a tremendous pace. As they reach the village the whole tribe swarm out like bees, and while the men are nocking their arrows and looking for a signal from the other party, and the women are screaming and pulling their children out of the way, they dash through, leaping over or capsizing whatever hinders, until they find themselves entirely clear. Glancing round they see the savages all standing talking excitedly, and looking after them, evidently in high dudgeon, but not attempting to pursue them farther.

They scarcely draw rein for the next ten miles, and then they pause to recruit their good steeds. It is plain now why their friends of yesterday were so anxious to change the direction of their journey, and they congratulate themselves on escaping so serious a danger.

CHAPTER VI.

SAVED.

A CAREFUL estimate of the distance they
have ridden, shows that it is now time to
leave the valley and steer westwards. On
turning to the right, to carry out his intention, the doctor declares that by the position of the sun they must be going in exactly the wrong direction. 'How so?'
asks Herbert: 'it is noon, and by leaving
the sun to the left we must be going to the
west.' The doctor is very positive, and at
length relieves his comrade's perplexity as
to the cause of the divergence of opinion,

by saying, ' Well, do as you like, but I am
quite sure that for the last twelve years I
have always considered that the sun at noon
is due north, and consequently—'

' Oh, I see,' cries Herbert, ' you think
yourself still in South America instead of
at forty degrees north latitude.'

After the hilarity that followed the discovery of the doctor's blunder, and the
suggestion that it would be a good thing if
people who differed could always as easily
comprehend each other's stand-point, they
commence to scale the mountain. The first
ascent is long and steep, and so weakened
are they by want of food, that they can
hardly drag themselves up. Towards
evening they look for a camping ground.
Down in a hollow appears a patch of grass
and water, but the only way to it is over
large slabs of granite, smooth and polished,
down which the horses slide with their feet
close together. After much difficulty and

risk they reach the bottom in safety. A
hare runs across their path, and Herbert
fires at it their last charge but one. Wound-
ing it in the leg, he flings himself off his
horse to catch it, but it is still too nimble,
and escapes. The horses again feed mag-
nificently on rich green grass that reaches
to their backs, so that they can stand and
fill themselves without stirring. After
measuring out their five teaspoonsful of
beans, the travellers lie down to sleep; the
doctor for the first time showing despondency. It is not food he cares for, but tobacco. So long as that lasted he didn't
care; and his pipe now has lost the very
flavour of tobacco. As for perishing in the
mountains, he says he does not so much
mind that. He is not responsible. Herbert
is guide, and that is his business. And as
for singing, Horace talked nonsense when
he said 'Cantabit vacuus.' He defies an
empty man to sing.

Herbert remarks that it was Juvenal who made that observation, but they do not talk much as they ride along, and when they do talk it is all about food. For some nights past their dreams have all been of magnificent banquets, and in the mornings they compare notes as to what they have been feasting on in their sleep. One day while still upon the mountain, they come to a small heap of something white, or rather pale yellow, lying on the ground. To their astonishment it proves to be flour, which has evidently been spilt there months ago. Carefully scraping it up, they obtain about a pound which is tolerably clean. In the evening they make it into a cake and proceed to eat it. It is so sour that Herbert cannot manage to swallow much of his share. The doctor is more fortunate and finishes it.

The ridge upon which they are travelling turns out to be only a spur of the main

range, and they have to descend and cross
a long stretch of low country where there
is not a drop of water. Hitherto they have
drunk freely at every spring, but now that
they cannot fill the vacuum even with water,
they learn that the pains of hunger are a
trifle compared with those of thirst.

What is that large animal in the distance? Surely not an ox? If so, there
must be not only water, but there is meat,
and there may be men, white men.

It is an ox, thin and lame, and feeding
near a river that flows eastwards : a river so
large and rapid that they must be still far
from its sources in the Sierra Nevada :—still
on the wrong side of the mountain, and
still very far from any white man's abode.

Matters indeed look bad, for they know
not where they are, and their whole stock
of food does not weigh a pound. Herbert
remembers having heard the emigrants
speak of a river called the 'Truckee' which

has to be crossed several times on the route from the western States to California.

If this is it, the great western train may pass somewhere near them; and this ox may have been abandoned by some party as too lame to travel farther. Its shyness, on their attempting to approach it, shows that it has been alone for some time.

Making an enclosure by passing their ropes round some trees they succeed in driving it in. Herbert makes a careful examination of his pistol. It is the last charge : and if that fails—.

The poor beast is very quiet and eyes him wistfully, as, standing by a tree, he leans the barrel against it, and looks steadily along it, aiming at the curl on the forehead. The doctor says in a low tone, ' Don't shoot him there, the skull is too thick for a pistol-shot. Take him sideways under the ear.' Herbert shifts his position, bringing his aim to bear on the back of the head just below the root of the ear, and pulls the trigger. With a convulsive start the ox falls dead, and the two famine stricken wanderers speak not a word, but look at each other with the aspect of men who have just escaped an imminent danger. The first steak proves too tough to be eaten: not unlikely, when the animal had lately come off a journey of two thousand miles over rocky mountains and salt deserts. They will try stewing. The coffee-pot is filled with small pieces, and boiled for several hours. The meat is still uneatably tough, and indescribably nauseous for the want of salt. By turns they keep the pot simmering all night. In the morning they might as well have attempted to eat their boots. Chopping it up into very small pieces, and bruising it between stones, they are able to get enough down to keep body and soul together. With a large piece in their saddle-bags they follow up the course of the river, the water of which is so cold, and the current so rapid, that they are persuaded it can contain no fish. Soon, tracks become abundant, first of cattle, then of wheels; and presently they come upon a broad dusty road, with signs of recent travel. Then the remains of a fire, and a date upon a tree, telling that emigrants have rested there that morning. Yes, there is no doubt of it. There is a train of waggons upon the road, and but a little way in advance. Pressing on eagerly, they soon come up with a large party of men 'nooning' beneath some trees. They are all eating their mid-day meal, and eye the two wanderers somewhat coldly.

'Can we buy food of you? for we are starving,' they ask, eyeing, not the men, but the bread in their hands.

'No, we are on short allowance ourselves,' is the answer. 'Where do you come from?' At first they are incredulous that Herbert and the doctor are from the diggings, and have been wandering for more than a month in the mountains. They take them for emigrants who have pushed ahead of their party, on the chance of their being able to sponge upon those whom they might overtake. For there is great scarcity of food among all the emigrants that season.

Once assured that they have really come from the mines the emigrants show them no little kindness. Each man breaks off a small piece from the bread he is eating, and gives it to them. A little contribution of coffee is made from each pannikin. They are about thirty in number, so that Herbert and the doctor make the best meal they have had for many a day. And now the emigrants ply them with questions about the mines.

They have come nearly two thousand miles by land to dig for gold. There are some sixty thousand on the way. The amount of provisions necessary for the journey has generally been underestimated, and famine and cholera have lined the road with graves. They are now at the gates of the golden hills. The whole region of California is before them. Any information which will enable them to get to work without delay on entering the country, will be most acceptable. Nay, if Herbert and the doctor will guide them to such a spot, they will gladly share their rations with them for the rest of the journey. Their desires being moderate, Herbert thinks he knows a locality which will suit them. So they journey on together, the doctor tending the sick and wounded, and happy in once more having something to put into his pipe. In ten days more, for bullock waggons travel slowly, the Sierra Nevada is crossed and Herbert has conducted them to a pleasant location near the lower Yuba,

where he has before found gold in sufficient quantities to yield four or five
dollars a day. His friends are well pleased
with the place, which is, however, hardly
rich enough to induce him to settle upon
it also. But the first thing to do is to
procure a supply of provisions, and recruit
their wasted bodies. And this the doctor
does with so much energy that he nearly
kills himself with a colic.

CHAPTER VII.

A LAST TRIAL.

THE autumn being by this time far
advanced, the two companions are no
sooner fit for work than they seek a spot
whereon to fix themselves for the winter.
Herbert wrote but few notes of this winter's
operations.   It seems to have been passed
in extraordinary hard work, far up in the
snowy ranges, sometimes by themselves,
sometimes with the aid of hired men.

Tolerably successful, they return in the
spring to the Bay, having narrowly escaped

being robbed of their winter's earnings at a road-side house.

On reaching San Francisco Herbert discovers that one of the houses in which he has deposited money has failed, leaving him but little better off for the last season's work. He finds also a letter from his father mentioning the Australian discoveries and the rapid development of that country in consequence, and offering him a small allowance if he will go there and abandon his 'vagabond' life. He reminds him also that his education and college testimonials will still be available, should he think proper to enter the ministry in that colony. Herbert writes a grateful acknowledgment, expressing his hope that he may still get on without burdening his family, and his satisfaction at knowing that his intention of going to Australia will meet with approbation at home; but he does not add that he is not ashamed to dig, but would rather starve than beg to be put into one of the priest's offices that he may eat a piece of bread! That thought he reserves for his private note-book, from which also the following extracts will serve to indicate the stage and direction of his mind's progress during that winter.

'Necessity does not vanish from the universe before the supremacy of Will. God *must* act for the best. Of various courses he is not at liberty to select that which is least for his own " glory." If at any period he has foreseen the whole future course of events, he can only carry it out without the change of one smallest item in the infinite programme. Although already realized in the divine imagination as exactly as if they had occurred, the events of eternity must yet be all re-enacted in their living reality. Surely, rather than this, it is easier to believe that the existing series of things is the actual first thought,

or life of God. " Matter is mind precipi-
tated ? " otherwise to the infinite foreknow-
ledge all is stale certainty : there is no
trust, and no hope. Man is happier than
God, for he does not know the future.
(Does the charm of curves consist in this,
that they prevent us from seeing all at
once ? for I entirely mistrust the associa-
tion theory.)

*　　　*　　　*　　　*

' A species of fatalism may be found in
music, or any other art. If the music be
what we call good, each note and phrase
follows its predecessor inevitably. There
is no choice about it. Any other would
seem forced and misplaced. Thus, all great
works are evolutions from some simple
theme, out of which they grow naturally
and necessarily in a unique and concordant
whole. As it is bad composition in which
any change can be made that is not for the
worse ; so in the chain of circumstances

from the beginning until now, no single
event could have been otherwise without
marring the effect and disposition of the
whole universe.

  *   *   *   *

'To be able to say that anything is
imperfect involves a knowledge of the end
for which it is designed. Do we know
our own end ?

' " For the glory of God," says the theologian, and so far with truth. But he
adds, " we do not fulfil that end as we
might and ought."

' How does he know that ? We cannot
call a work divine, unless it is adapted to
fulfil the divine purpose. The fact is that
men imagine for themselves an end, and
condemn the work for not answering the
end they have imagined. Man's God is
man, not God. If the end of creation be
the highest happiness of all its parts, and
that happiness is only attainable through

such a course of instruction or development as we find going on in the world,
who dare say that man falls short of fulfilling the divine intention ? Man's idea
of perfection is equilibrium, rest, annihilation. He would attain it at once, and
cease.

*　　*　　*　　*

' Is the initial chaos of human ignorance
struggling towards the light, more blame-
able for its excesses and blunders than the
primal chaos of the physical world ?

*　　*　　*　　*

' There is a uniformity in · the divine
method in nature; first, physical, then
moral order, each evolved gradually out
of primitive confusion. Being required
for further use, in the realization of future
perfectibility, the materials must not be
destroyed. They are not faulty ; they
have only not yet reached the highest development of which they are capable. It

is not part of the divine method to produce this at once. There is no real confusion; only an earlier stage of the process. Chaos is a fiction. We really mean
by it a condition of things not adapted for
man's well-being. " Embryo " better ex-
presses what is meant.

  *   *   *   *

‘ By perfection, whether here or elsewhere, is only meant the adaptation of
our nature to our conditions.

  *   *   *   *

‘ One of the men working for us this
winter, a sober, staid New Englander from
the State of Maine, is deeply impressed by
the accounts he has received from home
about a practice called " Spirit-rapping."
He tells the most wonderful stories of com-
munications received from the dead by the
medium of knocks upon the table, and
states that " quite a number " of Americans
believe in their reality and divinity. The

doctor scoffs most unmercifully at it all, and wonders how I can listen to such trash. He says it is "just like me; incredulous about what everybody else believes, and yet ready to swallow anything." I know that this is a charge often brought against sceptics. But I think the inconsistency is only apparent. I can listen with a mind open to conviction to narratives of the wonders of Mesmerism, or even this new Spirit-rapping, because so long as they claim nothing beyond the limits of nature, their phenomena come within our legitimate sphere of inquiry. But directly I hear assertions regarding anything pretending to be supernatural, my whole reason rises against it as an impossible monstrosity. Nature, with me, including all that is.

*   *   *   *

'Talking with the doctor about the distribution of gold, which has long puzzled me, he says that he has no doubt one of the agents has been ice. The country was once probably much colder, either from change of the earth's climate, or from having been once at a greater elevation, and may have contained such glaciers as he has seen in the Cordilleras of the Andes, which by grinding against the sides of the hills detach the surface materials, and transport without farther attrition whatever has been collected by the ice to the valleys below, and then, by melting, gently deposit it upon the surface of the soil. This is more probable than the common notion of the miners, that the gold has been thrown up from a volcano, and remains much where it has chanced to fall.'

BOOK V.

'My purpose holds
To sail beyond the sunset and the baths
Of all the western stars—
It may be that the gulfs will wash us down:
It may be we shall touch the Happy Isles.'

TENNYSON's 'Ulysses.'

CHAPTER I.

SOUTHWARDS HO!

From Herbert Ainslie's Journal.

AWAY from the land of vain labour and baffled hope. Away from the land where the elements of human society yet seethe and boil up in reckless violence and un-mitigated self-seeking. Away, still far-ther away from the home of my youth. Ten thousand miles away, yet onward still! A new and, perchance, a better world beckons me towards it,—the New World of the South Seas. There, among my own countrymen, will I renew my quest; there seek the means of returning once more to see the inmates of the old home. Wherefore this perpetual clinging to home ? Is it thus with all men, even when provided with wife and children and interests to absorb them ? Home must be ever the place of the dearest ties; and I have no new ties: therefore am I lonely, and cling to the old memories. It seems as if one must have concrete personal attachments. I want rest, for I am very weary. This voyage will renew my strength. A new world, without one face I have ever seen before, needs some fulness of hope and energy to confront it. Ah me! would heaven be heaven without some of the old faces to cluster round, and smile a welcome on one's arrival ? There can be no heaven while still full of regrets for those left behind, and none to greet us there.

* * * *

Beneath the soft trade winds we are gliding over smooth seas rarely divided by a keel, in a capital yacht-like little craft, whose three owners—an Englishman, an Irishman, and a Frenchman, are all on board. It is laden with a cargo of varieties, with which they intend to trade with some of the islands for such articles as palm oil, tortoiseshell, sandal-wood, and beche-le-mer, the latter being a sort of sea-slug, which, when manufactured into soup, is esteemed a huge delicacy by Chinese Mandarins. All these things find a ready market in Sydney; and to that capital of the southern ocean are we bound, when the Island cruise and its purpose are accomplished. My companions are agreeable, especially the Frenchman, who is a lively little fellow, with a good deal of enthusiasm. Time goes as in a dream. There is just enough of consciousness to feel the work of renovation going on. I have one book with me, purchased in San Francisco, which is to me a new Apocalypse. It is

Bailey's poem of 'Festus.' Over this I ponder with a degree of delight almost equal to that with which I first read Carlyle's 'Hero Worship' in the Bay of Biscay. It seems to me that all my greatest pleasures have been derived from books. The first work of imagination beyond the ordinary reading of children that I remember, was Southey's 'Thalaba.' It was to me superhuman. No mere mortal, I thought, could possess such a faculty of imagining. The next work, after a long interval, that intensely attracted me was 'Jane Eyre.' In it I learned to appreciate the sanctity of the affections, and their superiority over mere conventionality. Then the 'Hero Worship,' suggesting the possibility of the divine in the human idea. Bulwer's 'Caxtons' next strangely affected me. It has been the tenant of my saddle-bags in many a long ride, and for months I cared to read nothing else. The two noble brothers, so simple, and high, and pure; the beauty of the relation between the father and the son; and the wondrous delicacy of the scene where the former details his own most painful experiences for his boy's benefit, touched me so that even now I am unable to read the book aloud. Would that all fathers established the same relations with their children. And now 'Festus' is my bible; no other book ever 'found' me, to use Coleridge's phrase, in so many parts of my nature. And this is the only proof we have of the truth, whether in a book or in anything else,—the finding oneself in it. No revelation could be inspired for us unless it coincided with our nature and wants; and if it does thus coincide with humanity, why should it not be a human product? To this list I must add Emerson's Essays, which have been for me a never-failing spring of refreshing, and fountain of wisdom.

*   *   *   *

The sensation of indolent contentment
fostered by this kind of life in these latitudes is very pleasant.   I find it singularly
antagonistic to all ideas of duty or ambition.
Under its prolonged influence I can fancy
myself becoming an oyster,—another proof
of the identity of perfection and negation.
Yet I am not without much to think about;
nor are my companions undeserving of a
niche in my note-book.

The English owner is also our captain ; a good-natured fellow in act, though
of the most dogged contradictory disposition in words.   Nothing can be said in a
simple conversation that does not excite
his combativeness.   At last, guessing the
secret of his universal opposition, I asked
him, during one of its exhibitions, if, supposing he were clearly shown to his own
satisfaction to be wrong, he would own

it ;—' No,' he replied, ' I'd die first.'

The Frenchman is a curious compound (though not curious perhaps for a Frenchman) of volatility and earnestness. He is as thoroughly free from any prepossession in favour of Christianity, as if he had been born in a Turkish Hareem.

He has carried his acquaintance with the ancient mythologies to a remarkable extent, and has come to regard Christianity as but a refined Pagan eclecticism. He admires the prudence of the Romish Church in keeping the original records of their faith out of sight, on the ground that people will not be long content to read the Bible without investigating the history of its composition, ' and when once they do that, adieu to Christianism.'

For Protestantism he has a vast contempt, as ' the product of an unnatural alliance between faith and knowledge; a hybrid compounded of equal parts of darkness and light, having no vital principle of its own, and only possible as a transition to one or the other extreme.'

In his view, 'Priestism' is stronger in modern Europe than ever it was in old times, for 'the priests have thrown away the keys, and have come to believe their own lie at least many of them do.' The only religion he professes is that of ' Solidarité,' or community of interest, which he confidently expects sooner, or later, to take the place of all other principles of action. His imperfect English and lively manner are very piquant.

' When any person tries to Christianize me, I say to them, "Beware ! you are a Novice, and I am one of the Initiated. Will you, who are only allowed to enter the outer court, teach a high priest who has been behind the veil, and seen all the holy mysteries?" And when they contend that they are indeed true believers, I do beam on them and cry out "Ah, you have a good heart." But I do not tell them what I know, for it is good for them to think true what they teach ; and if I convert them they would lose their good heart (i. e. act dishonestly), or they would starve ; and it is pain to me when people starve or have a bad heart.'

His theory is that every religion was originally a worship of the sun, and that Christianity is the product of a union between certain astronomical and philosophical conclusions. In support thereof he enumerates some curious parallelisms.

Hercules, Apollo, Bacchus, Æsculapius, and other classical divinities, the Hindoo Chrishna, the Egyptian Osiris, Pythagoras, and the Jewish Christ, he regards as being all mere personifications of the Sun ; and won't hear of any of the details which their histories have in common, being derived from the Gospels. Quoting the prophecy of

Æsculapius in Ovid's Metamorphoses, he exhibits the identity of its details with what afterwards was believed by Christians. He adduces also Justin Martyr's acknowledgment that the Christians claimed little more for their Jesus than the Pagans for their Æsculapius : and states that to him also were applied the epithets of 'God the Saviour,' the 'healer of men,' and 'conqueror of death.' He makes a great point of the coincidence between the creed and the course of the Sun ; how that it passes through the constellation Virgo ; descends below the earth ; rises again and ascends into heaven ; revealing the kingdom of heaven, that is, day or summer. The twelve apostles through which his light is spread, are the twelve months ; Judas being February which ' transgresses,' or passes over a day, and so falls into his proper place. (Is there a more intelligible interpretation of Acts i. 25 ?)

More curious still is the astrological function he assigns to John the Baptist, the patron or ' génie' of June 24th. He considers him as regarding from one pole of the year the infant Jesus, the ' génie ' of December 25th. At the other pole, the saying of John, ' He must increase, but I must decrease,' having reference to the fact that the days begin to lengthen from Christmas day, and to shorten from June 24th. To the shortest day, December 21st, is assigned the doubting apostle Thomas as patron : for then the year, having reached the lowest depths of its darkness, may be supposed to fear lest its Lord, the Sun, can never rise again.

Besides Voltaire, whom he styles ' the greatest of Biblical critics,' there is an English book, he tells me, in which I can find all this and a vast deal more concerning the origin of Christianity well worked out. The author was a ' Marteer,' whose name he thinks was Taylor.

According to his theory, the calendar should be reversed in the southern hemisphere.

It is very certain that the subject of Christian Evidences has not been dealt fairly with. The selection of any one period of history, however remote, and the collation of all that is known or believed about it, must necessarily cause the period and the events ascribed to it to stand out distinctly and separately from the surrounding time and circumstances, and to assume a prominence by no means properly belonging to them. So that what is in reality a single link in a great chain of transitions, may thus be made to outweigh and eclipse the whole series of facts to which it belongs.

What we require is a history of philosophy and religion at the time immediately prior to the origin of Christianity.

In short, I want to see the human history of the world dealt with as geologists are dealing with the Earth's physical history.

Theologians seem to think that Catastrophe is the only possible evidence of divine handiwork, and that if all things went on smoothly and without jerks, the Universe would afford no proof of God's existence. But it is probably only because we have knowledge of the results merely of different eras, and not of the details of the periods of transition that connect them, that the notion has grown up that history has jumped from one summit, as it were, to another, and that each complete period has been the product of a separate miraculous action, instead of having grown naturally out of the periods which have preceded it. The progress of Geology is certainly tending towards this conclusion in respect to the earth, and I am strongly inclined to think

that if we only could get at the real history
of the period between the Old and New
Testaments, and especially that of the condition of Judæa and its relation to Egypt
and to Egyptian schools of thought at the
time of Christ's birth, we should find that
He was as much a natural product of his
age and country as any other representative man.

The vicious habit of restricting history
to kings and wars, may account for the
scantiness of our knowledge on this head,
but it is not unlikely that the founders of
the Ecclesiastical System destroyed, or at
least willingly suffered to perish, very
many documents that would have thrown
light on this subject, and that it is to the
design of those founders rather than to the
facts themselves, that Christianity owes
its apparent preternatural isolation and in-
dependence. As they held that the Earth
leaped into being from the void, so they

represent Christianity as having suddenly
started into existence out of a complete
blank ; like the tremendous winter of
Northern America out of the dreamy hush
of the 'Indian Summer' that precedes it.

Very curious is the effect of this Frenchman's conversation on these subjects.
Listening to his enumeration of one coincidence after another between the fables of
Pagan Mythology and the traditions of the
Church, the character of Jesus comes to appear so shadowy and legendary that there
would be little difficulty in disbelieving
any such person to have existed at all, were
it not for the impossibility of otherwise ac-
counting for the ascription of these relations
to one of his era and nation.

I agree with him that these questions
must all be reopened in order to be settled
one way or the other. They have never
really been settled, but only ignored, and
inquiry denounced. He says there is evi-

dence enough to convince any unbiassed
mind, notwithstanding that the successful
majority in the early ages of the Church
always destroyed as much as they could of
the evidences brought against them.

CHAPTER II.

THE HAPPY ISLES.

WE glide on as in a pleasant dream. Such days, such nights of beauty. We have passed the sun, and our noon-day shadows point to the south. Higher and higher in the nightly sky rides the Southern Cross; soon will the Southern Isles appear. An end to dreaming now, for much caution is necessary to thread with safety the coral labyrinths of these seas. Sometimes in a moment the deep blue of fathomless ocean gives place to an almost milky white, and at a short distance appears a cluster of

little circles of coral, presenting their rims
just above the water, and looking like so
many white fairy rings enclosing lagoons of
stillest water.   This when the sea is calm;
but in boisterous weather the waves dash
madly over them, and woe to the ship that
is cast upon their teeth.   Rings, then
indeed, they prove, to wed the unhappy
mariner to his death.   One, two, islands
are passed, mere knolls of palm trees, apparently growing out of the ocean.   At
last higher land appears in sight.   A few
hours more and we glide along a reef-
bound shore, catching glimpses of lovely
valleys in among hills covered with unfad-
ing green.   Soon we descry a movement
on the land, and a canoe comes off, paddled by half a dozen natives, and steered
by a white man.   This is a pilot, who has
lived half a life in these seas.   He guides
us through an opening in the reef, between
the long lines of surf, to a safe anchorage

in still water. It is so clear, that gazing many a fathom down we can see the branching coral of white and red, and gaily coloured fishes darting about, or pausing among the boughs as birds in a tree.

Now we are surrounded by canoes laden with tropical fruits and poultry, and are deafened by the clamour of the natives, rich copper-coloured fellows, girt with cinctures of sea-weed. A noble-looking race, with handsome Grecian features, and pleasant, gentle manners. I get into a canoe and am paddled ashore, with the little Frenchman. It is a beautiful little bay, edged with a narrow strip of white beach which slopes down to waters ever smooth and clear; for the encircling reef keeps afar off the roar and tumult of ocean. The shore is lined with groves of orange and citron, bananas, cocoa-nut, and bread-fruit trees. Under the shade of these are ranged the huts of the natives, spacious and well-built. Walking down to meet us on our landing, comes a fair girl of some fifteen summers, or rather of one summer fifteen years long, and beautiful as a dream, with soft dark eyes, and long glossy black ringlets hanging down her glowing shoulders, and revealing a bust and figure of most perfect form. Her smooth shining skin is of lighter hue than the other natives. She is clad with the prevailing cincture of weeds from the waist nearly to the knees, and is now in the full perfection of fresh womanhood and beauty. Serene and dignified as an empress, and yet purely artless and unconscious, she advances towards us. I think of 'vera incessu patuit Dea;' and the little Frenchman throws up his arms and exclaims—

'This *is* an Arabian Night.'

There are missionaries and other white men on the island, so she may have learnt a little English.

'What is your name?'

'Maleia,' is the response, in soft Samoan accents; for we are upon the island of
Opolo, one of the Navigator's or Samoa
group. Beautiful Maleia thus understanding me, we soon become friends, and I
decorate her fair neck with some trinkets I
had been careful to bring with me. Di-
rected by her, the little Frenchman seeks
the abodes of the white men; and she
leads me in search of fruit to the adjoining
banana grove. Evidently a kind and
gentle-hearted damsel, though very sparing
of her words: comprehending pretty well
what I say, but averse to answering except
in her native Samoan; a singularly soft
language, in which it is difficult to detect
any consonants. Here Maleia selects for
me the finest bananas, and when I have
enough of these, shakes down a green cocoa-
nut, and opening it carefully, gives me a
draught of milk, sweet, refreshing, and

delicious. The white kernel is soft as thick cream, very different from the hard indigestible stuff so dear to British school-boys. Here, reclining under the great banana leaves, the moist and balmy air, laden with fragrance and indescribable richness, throws a mantle of oblivion over all the past, shrouding all its cherished schemes in far indistinctness, and inducing a longing to dream away the remainder of life undisturbed alike by regret and desire. Here one learns to sympathize with Adam in his garden of delights, and to feel that he would have been a heartless wretch, what Yankees call ' a mean man,' had he refused the apple at Eve's hand. He would have shown a fussy moral activity inconsistent with any largeness of nature, and with the serene influence of the place; and a ready consciousness of evil that ill harmonized with real innocence.

*   *   *   *

Maleia has told me her history. She is proud to claim kindred with white men, for her father is one. When quite a baby he left her to the care of her native mother and the missionaries. She must move homeward now for the day is nearly done. Even as we thread our way through the grove, the sun is gone, and as we pace along the smooth white beach the heavens burst into stars. The very sea does the same, for the clear reef-bound waters, free from all motion, reflect each orb in lustre unbroken and undiminished. O Poet, I have realized thy dream! and until sleep comes that night, do the luscious stanzas of ' Locksley Hall ' ring in my ears, making sweetest harmony with the time and the place. Yes, I too have

' Burst all links of habit, and have wandered far away,
  On from island unto island, at the gateways of the day.

' Larger constellations burning, mellow moons and
    happy skies,

Breadth of tropic shade, and palms in cluster, knots
  of paradise.

' Drops the heavy blossomed bower, hangs the heavy
    fruited tree,
  Summer isles of Eden lying in dark purple spheres
    of sea.

' Here the passions, cramped no longer, shall have
    scope and breathing space ;
  I will take some savage woman, she shall rear my
    dusky race.'

And perchance this glorious dusky
damsel, more beautiful than ever poet
dreamed, will not refuse to fulfil her part
in the destiny !

CHAPTER III.

CHRISTIAN AND CANNIBAL.

NEXT morning I wander on shore again, and while the owners busy themselves in traffic, I find out some of the missionaries, and chat with them. Pleasant, easy-going men, sent out by the great London Society. Living in comfortable European-fashioned houses, with wives and pale-looking children, wishing for nothing but a little more society. Instantly noticeable is the utter absence of the chronic excitement which pervades all missionary reports. One does not talk long with them without perceiv-

ing that they have settled down, and that
somewhat listlessly, to their work, with
minds little occupied by expectation of
ever making anything of the islanders;
who, they say, readily acknowledge the
superiority of the white man, and learn to
imitate his habits even to the details of
church ceremony.

Looking into the chapel on Sunday,
I see this for myself. Everything is done
in the decorous English meeting-house
fashion. The service is in the native
tongue. Some two hundred are present,—
but a small portion of the population,—
dressed in what they consider their Sunday best. Generally huge rolls of tappa,
a white native cloth, looking Roman and
graceful enough, were it not for the addition of English incongruities—a tawdry
bonnet or coloured shirt. As with all
savages, as well as with some who do not
profess to be in the least savages, their

weak side is dress. Of course, in order to acquire influence over them the missionaries must act upon such motives as they find to exist. And going to the mission chapel is a duty paramount over all the harmony and beauty in the world. Their imitativeness is shown in the service. There is the average amount of apparent attention ; the usual absence of all enthusiasm or eagerness ; tolerable singing of hymns, and an orderly departure when all is over ; and even the same appearance of relief as from a task performed.

Even to the abstinence of the chapel-goers from other appearance in public on Sunday, is everywhere notable the aim to patch with cold northern formalism the garb of unconscious simplicity hitherto by nature deemed sufficient for these islanders. Beholding this wherever the missionary influence extends, I feel annoyed. Why always this trying to prevent people from being themselves, and to make them some one else quite different ?

Close by the mission chapel is the grave of the first missionary to these islands, John Williams, who after many years of successful adventure against idol-worship, met. his death in 'tempting Providence' by rashly venturing alone among a tribe fiercer than any he had before visited. Interesting stories the missionaries tell me of the conversion of these Samoans. It seems that they were always a race of gentle manners, and though not unwarlike, generally eschew human flesh. One of the islands, Manono, though by no means the largest, claims a sort of political superiority over the whole group. Enclosed within the same reef, it is so easy of access from Opolo that the inhabitants have often been surprised and driven from their island.

On these occasions· they betake themselves to a natural fortress that at a short distance from their shores rises abruptly from the sea. This is a rock, steep, rugged, and barren : a hopeless-looking spot as one approaches it, and sails round and round without seeing any opening whereby the interior can be gained. A passage, however, there is, narrow and overhung by precipices. But on entering this, the scene changes as by magic. The rock is a hollow basin, of which the whole inside at once appears, sloping regularly and gently from the centre up to the edge of the encircling hill, and all covered with most glorious verdure of food-yielding trees, with here and there clusters of native dwellings resting under their shades. It is evidently the crater of an extinct volcano, and is aptly termed by the Samoans, Aborima,— the hollow of the hand. Accessible only by the narrow and easily-defended aperture in the lip of the volcano, and bountifully

supplied with food and water, Aborima
is proof against the attacks both of man
and of the elements. The hurricane sweeps
in vain round its rugged sides, while the
low and sheltered centre rests undisturbed.
In a motionless atmosphere, and with a
vertical sun, the heat would here be in-
tolerable, were it not that the whole climate
of these islands is deliciously tempered by
the constant tradewinds. The interest of
Manono for the missionary is due to the
circumstance that it was mainly instru-
mental in bringing about the abandonment
of the old religion by the Samoans. Its
old chief, Malietoa, after listening to the
accounts given by the missionaries of the
superiority of 'Jehovah' to the gods of
the islanders, and seeing the many conveniences possessed by his followers, determined to put the matter to a test that
to him appeared conclusive. Calling his
people together, he told them that in

order to try whose gods were the strongest, he intended to worship 'Jehovah' for six weeks. And if at the end of that time no calamity had befallen him, they should all become Christians. This was agreed to. And during the period of probation the excitement is said to have been intense; bulletins being constantly despatched to all parts of the island, announcing the progress of the contest between the rival deities. Before the time had half expired, the people, who were already well disposed towards the whites, were tired of waiting, and the proposed change was made at once. The missionaries themselves, who had not objected to the test, coolly accepted the safety of Malietoa as proof of their God's interference and omnipotence. They admit that if anything had happened to him, their own lives would have been sacrificed. It is little wonder that a religion thus rested on a certain supernatural action, should be endangered when other supposed supernatural action less favourable in its character occurred.

A subsequent series of calamities, sickness, fire, and hurricane, was of course interpreted by the natives as proofs of the displeasure of their old gods at being forsaken. Many relapsed into heathenism, and it required all the wit of the missionaries to counteract the hostile feeling. In doing this they were much aided by the presents they were able to make out of their stores of a variety of European tools, axes, saws, &c., articles of which all savages have an intense appreciation.

At first sight it would seem as if the missionaries practised a wilful deceit upon the natives, in representing all the advantages and conveniences of civilization as boons bestowed upon them by 'Jehovah' in return for their preference of Him to other gods, when, by a truer statement, it would appear that the same acuteness of intellect that led them to have higher ideas of God, or, which is nearly the same thing, ideas of a higher God, would also enable them to invent superior appliances of physical comfort.   But the belief in special providences is so interwoven with their whole system of thought, that they appear quite unconscious of the misapprehensions concerning the connection between the operations of the elements and their own religious belief, which they foster in the native mind.   I do not, however, interrupt their narratives or disturb their complacency with any such reflections of my own.

The various English societies, they tell me, have agreed not to interfere with each other's fields of operation, and, no doubt, they are wise in this, for the native mind will quite soon enough discern difficulties and inconsistencies in the doctrines of their teachers, without their being paraded before them by a diversity of sects. In Opolo, however, are a couple of French priests, who have been for some time trying to gain sway over the natives, though as yet with but little success. Even more incongruous than the formalism of the English missionaries appear these men, in their long black serge habits. One of them is styled bishop, and the chapel he is building of hewn blocks of white coral is called cathedral. They seem to care more to convert Protestants into Romanists, than cannibals into Christians; perhaps because it is the more difficult task.

CHAPTER IV.

LOTOS EATING.

PLEASANT is it to get away from all these signs of ' civilization,' and mix with the yet unsophisticated natives. Not that they are without strange, and even absurd customs of their own. The men, for instance, hold their hair in high reverence, and it is a profanation to touch it. They delight to make each hair stand straight out from the head, like that of an electric doll when excited. They put lime upon it, which turns it of a reddish hue. Just after our arrival, I found the Irish owner declaiming against the impertinence of some natives, who were greatly attracted by his flaming locks, and begged to know his recipe for making it that beautiful colour. He thought they were making fun of him. Near the village, filtering through the beach into the sea, is a beautiful little stream of purest water, in which the whole population bathes two or three times a day. A little way back it becomes a considerable pool, over-shadowed by large trees. This is a scene of huge merriment and delight, when, crawling along the overhanging limbs, men and boys come dropping down in swarms, and diving away to marvellous distances. Every one swims. Mothers take their babies in with them, and the little things paddle away long before they can walk. No troublesome toilette for any of us after bathing. The slight amount of clothing required by the climate is no inconvenience to either man or woman in

swimming.   A shirt, duck-trousers, and
shoes I find both ample and picturesque.
Maleia and I are great friends.   Somehow,
she is rarely far off.   She comes early from
her home, in one of the mission-houses, to
be my companion and guide in the intricate
ways through the banana groves to the
neighbouring villages.   I find tobacco
everywhere the welcomest present, and
therefore carry some with me.   Every
family possesses its own plot of ground,
containing the staple food of life,—bread-
fruit and cocoa-nut trees.   The former is
a most beautiful tree, in largeness of leaf
and depth of colour resembling, but exceeding, the fig.   It is to the islanders
what the cow is to the European ; all parts
of it serving some necessary end.   The
natives generally place their huts close to
one or more of them ; and in their shade
we rest on arriving at any village, and I
dispense my tobacco, and we all smoke a

friendly pipe, Maleia herself not disdaining
the delicate paper cigarita. Sometimes,
in a light canoe, we paddle at evening
along the inner side of the reef, to see the
fishing by torch-light. The topmost edge
of the reef is level with the water, and a
perpetual surf breaks upon it. A strange
effect is produced by the dark figures of
the natives, with spear in one hand and a
blazing torch of reeds in the other, tread-
ing the white lines of foam, which gleam
and flash brightly in the moving lights,
as, with many a shout and splashing into
deep water, they alternately attract and
scare the fish into becoming an easy prey.

Maleia herself swims like a mermaid, so
that, when wandering on shore, the rivers
do not impede us; for, hand in hand, we
tread the depths, and merrily pass to the
other side. And when I have been away
with my trading companions, cruising
among the islands that skirt the horizon, I

am always sure of a bright look from her on my return.

Between two of the islands there is war. From the schooner-decks I witness a hostile invasion. Paddling over in immense canoes, the enemy attempt to land. A combat ensues, partly on shore, partly on the water and in the water. With spears, and darts, and clubs, the attempt is repulsed; and, laden with the 'casualties,' the canoes paddle back in mournful procession to whence they came. There will be much lamentation on their return, for a great chief is slain. None of the old horrors are now enacted with the prisoners; so far has twenty years' contact with white men mitigated their cruelty. In fighting and dancing they find their chief excitements. The missionaries have done their best to discourage both; but where the physical energies have so long been alone exercised, it is not easy to arouse the mental, or to

make intellectual pursuits successful rivals
of the animal, even if the missionaries were
the right men for the task.

*   *   *   *

How absurd to judge these children of
the sun by the ascetic standard of the
cold north !   No necessity for effort is here
to sharpen their wits.   Friction denied,
how can they make progress ?   No harsh
climate impels to the accumulation of com-
forts.   Their food springs spontaneously
from the earth, and all they have to do is
to enjoy its bounties and continue their
race.   I find myself looking back with
wonder to the old world, and its life of
anxious wear and tear ; its hastening to be
rich, its emulation between man and man,
and its vast interval between the extremes
of life.   If heaven be conscious rest, surely
I have it here,—so delightful from its contrast with the weary past !   Why should I
ever leave it ?   Where shall I find a simpler

solution of the problem of life than among
these careless islanders? Are they so ' low
in the scale'? Surely it is envy that has
so placed them. They stretch forth their
hands for fruit, and are filled. They drink
at the stream, and are satisfied. They
know no cold, and if heat assail them they
have but to lie still in the thick shade of
their trees. They love, and have children;
and sickness makes little havoc in their
dwellings. They can avenge injuries, be
grateful for kindness, and give thanks for
their blessings according to their knowledge; for their religious rites, uncouth
and childish though they seem to strangers,
do certainly not spring from ingratitude.
What conditions, then, are wanting to
make the traditionary Eden? The most
innocent children playing in a garden will
occasionally squabble, and enact uncon-
sciously many antics that, to the self-re-
garding, deliberate man, seem horrible

distortions.   Alas, that their guilelessness is doomed, and that European serpents should come so far to convince them of sin !

Surely I have reached the Happy Isles.

' How weary seems the sea,—the wandering fields of barren foam.   I will return no more.   My island home is far beyond the sea.   No longer will I roam.'

Why should I ?   The soft influences of the place are lulling to sleep all intellectual energy.   My physical being is renewed by every breath I inhale.   All impulses are becoming sensuous.   I toss up my cap and cry, ' *Vive la bête !* '

CHAPTER V.

A FAREWELL.

'So soon! how the weeks have flown.'
' Yes, there is no more cargo to be got in
the Navigator's, so to-morrow we sail, and
after touching at the Feejees, make straight
course for Port Jackson, and white English
faces again.'

The delight of my comrades at the
prospect startles me as from a dream.
Thoughts of the long-cherished plans of
busy life, ambition, and the return home
some day, crowd upon me. Is the old
Adam still so strong in me drawing me
towards my kindred?

Shall I go or stay? Malcia has taught
me what it is I want to fulfil the comple-
ment of my nature. To remain and live
with her—how great a happiness—and she
is willing. How selfish I shall appear to
her! It never occurred to me that she was
old enough to have feelings also. How
inexplicable to her wild simple nature
must be the feelings that call me away!
Will it be for the happiness of either if I
remain? Will the future be in accordance
with the present? Can she ever respond
to aught but the simple pleasures known
to her race, or sympathize with the higher
and more complex emotions of which I
feel capable? Ah me, I fear me it is too
plain. This would not be the perfect
marriage of which I have dreamt; in
which all parts of my nature, moral, intellectual, as well as physical, can meet
perfect sympathy and accord. I must not
linger here. It is not the highest thing I

can do. This is but the gateway of the day. The dawn has come, discovering to me my want. But the day does not stand still. I must press on to the full fruition and accomplishment of my higher nature.

So far with regard to myself:—but Maleia. True and natural as she is, she will not conceal her sorrow. Young and light-hearted, probably no feeling can be very deep-seated. I will tell her that it would be for the happiness of neither of us for me to remain. She would soon discover that there is little really in common between us, and feel a longing for the companionship of one of her own race: and I should feel that I was neglecting duties elsewhere, and be unhappy in the thought.

     *   *   *   *

I have told her this. With a quiet thoughtful air she listened as if not fully comprehending me, and then said, first proudly,

'Maleia got white blood too. Maleia no Samoan;' then sadly and reproach-fully,

'Why go when you fond of Maleia? Go when you tired of her.'

And this is all she said until I reached the end of my explanations, when she re-plied, 'Maleia no understand, but Maleia sorry.'

I wonder if I am a brute. I am sure I did not mean to be one. I am another proof that

> 'Evil is wrought by want of thought,
> As well as by want of heart.'

CHAPTER VI.

COOLING REFLECTIONS.

In the interval before reaching the
Feejees, Herbert solaces himself with his
note-book. The islands and the missionaries afford much to be reflected upon.
The following seems to consist as much of
his after-thoughts as of actual conversations :—

'The English are a greater and a better
people than you Samoans. By doing as
the English do, you too will become
greater and better.'

'Very doubtful to me is this first assertion of yours, as I think of our reeking manufacturing dens of great English cities, and contrast them with this paradise of ease and simplicity. And as for your second, ah, friend missionary, is this all you know of nature and her many types? Would you feed with oats and put saddle on yonder fat pigs of yours, because a horse is "greater and better" than a pig? Believe me, the pig has his place and his uses in it. Would you turn all the wild roses into vegetables? Even with individual men, each man should be himself, not the copy of another, however admirable in his line that other may be. And so with races of men. I know you say every one ought to try to be like Christ. No doubt, but not as you mean. Rather in being his own best; in acting up to the best that he finds in him, even as Christ did. Truly you cannot find a better example. As he acted out his own character, so ought we to act

out ours; to be true and natural and not
ape others. For the perfection of nature
consists in infinite variety of patterns, and
in their harmony with the conditions surrounding them. She loves not to see frogs
striving to become oxen. Say you, if one
be right all others must be wrong? In the
Absolute, concerning which we can know
nothing, it may be so. But in man, and
his circumstances, I see it not. Would
you exhort the reed to follow the example
of the oak, to be strong, and unyielding,
and a tree? Would you have quaker-like
rainbows, all one colour, which is no
colour? Why not? if red be a right
colour, blue is a wrong one. And if Nature delights in a rainbow of human varieties, would you charge her with bad taste,
and spoil her handiwork by abolishing the
variety?'

'Place and fitness?'

'Truly we begin to be agreed; but you

ask what you would have us do. How
make Christians of these savages? How
make them believe in the one Name given
under heaven whereby they can be saved?
Can you not do all this, make them Christian or Christ-like without bonnets and
breeches? How have you gone to work?
as I have read in your publications (for be
it known to you that I too come of evangeli-
cal stock and was fearfully bored with your
reports in my youth)—by denunciation of
everything you found, themselves, and
their habits, and their religion, and their
laws. Nothing good, no not one. And so
your whole experience is one of difficulty
and discouragement. Methinks, if I had
been a missionary, it would have been my
satisfaction to recount how that when I
had gone among tribes who had never seen
a white man, I told them that in the
farthest part of the round earth I had
heard that they knew and believed things

different from what I knew and believed; and that if they would teach them to me I would teach them in turn what they did not know, so that the exchange might be for the benefit of both. How that on see-ing their idol-worship I told them that my people also resembled them in this, distant and unlike as they were in many things. For that we too had a consciousness of a powerful Being whom we could not see, to whom we gave such offerings as we be-lieved to be pleasant to him. And, on thus discovering that they already pos-sessed a religious faculty, and could com-prehend my meaning, I was careful not to abuse but to use this faculty, and en-deavoured to cultivate it, and so lead them up gradually to a higher ideal of faith and worship, not by the assertion of things strange and incomprehensible to them, but by the development of that which they already had. And when I saw them fighting, killing, and eating each other, I took the opportunity to tell them that where I came from there were creatures called wild beasts, which their beautiful islands were quite free from, and that we left these brutes to do all such barbarous things, and were ashamed to imitate them. That the white men aimed at being happy, and making others so, and to that end laboured to discover all the secrets of the world, to turn them to good account. That instead of attributing any misfortune that befalls them to a malignant deity, they should regard it rather as a consequence of their own mistakes, or as a necessary part of a scheme which, on the whole, works for their good; like that last terrible hurricane, which, though it destroyed their habitations and cocoa-nut trees, yet cleared away the disease which was killing their children, the disease itself being the natural consequence of their own neglect or ignorance. That actual phenomena were not the capricious acts of their deities, but were consequences necessarily connected together, affording them fitting exercise for their faculties in extracting the good, or avoiding the mischief they brought. That instead of fierce, ugly demons, we worshipped one more like what we ourselves wished to be; a powerful and benevolent Being, believing that every quality we esteemed best belonged to him in the highest degree. That long ago our fathers had made and worshipped images just as they did now, but had learnt that none could be made like God, who was better understood by the things that he had himself made; by the sun and stars, the earth and all the beautiful and grand things upon it, by human souls and bodies, and the great powers of nature; but that the best likeness was the best man, and so we reverenced that the most

of all things, and worshipped none but
God himself as we saw him in our own
highest thought; while each one of us
tried to be the best man according to our
disposition and ability. And I doubt not
that I should have to finish my story by
telling how that these savages listened,
and thought it would be better, instead of
destroying each other and practising cruel
ceremonies, to help in securing their crops,
and to have their wives and children safe,
and to live in harmony together with
joyous festivals and dances; never fighting
but when they were attacked, and then
showing their enemies that they only
wished to be left in quiet.

'Do you, friend missionary, say that
your zeal for God would prevent your
treating idol-worship with such soft words?
Methinks you would more effectually
destroy it than by the means you have
employed. The only way to destroy an

error is to show that it is an error, and how
it is an error ; and to make its holders
understand how something else is better.
So far as I can see, you have not done
this. You have not shown them in what
the Christian doctrine is better suited to
their needs than their own. You have
simply taken advantage of your prestige
as white men to declare that your talisman
is better than their talisman, that your
fetich is Christ, and is stronger than their
fetich. Of the inherent excellence of your
system you have taught them nothing.
But what, after all, is this same idol-worship
for which you have such wholesome horror
and indignation, but a misdirection of the
religious faculty ; misdirection through
ignorance ? Can you be sure that the
sacrifice of these poor heathen is not accepted even as the widow's mite, in that
they do their best, and act up to the light
that is in them ? Do you say that they

seem rather to do their worst ? I fear me
ye be but blind leaders of the blind. Are
not all men inevitably attracted by that
which seems best to them ? You think to
make them Christians without cultivating
their intelligence. All you wish to do is
to get them to substitute your dogmas for
their own. Beware lest when you have
taken away their gods, and taught them to
pay reverence to a name, they continue to
worship under the new name the very
same idea that they worshipped in the old
image. Without a real accession of intelligence, a development of the idea of excellence, the image is but transferred from
the bodily sight to the mind's eye. So
that if idolaters before, they are idolaters
still, even when worshipping in your mission chapel. What but children are they,
with fair capacity and full of rude force ?
You would not treat a child's intellectual
blunders with harsh denouncement. You

would strive by gentle degrees to enlarge
his understanding and teach him better.
If religion be what some have defined it,
"man bringing to his Maker the homage of
his heart," least of all would a father re
probate his child for showing its reverence
to him in some foolish, childish mode, so
long as it did it out of reverence. It
might be different if the child did not
reverence its parent;—if the savage was
not even an idolater. Though in the
former case we should blame the parent
either for having concealed himself from
his child, or for having treated it so as to
forfeit its regard. And in the latter how
much you would think gained if the savage
became an idolater : just as you would regard it as a vast step in the scale of intelligence on the part of any animal, were it
to show its consciousness of a superior
being by laying its homage and offerings
before an image of it. And, after all, this

horror of yours towards images is only a dogmatic sentiment. It is adopted and not real. When you want to make an idea clear to a child, if words fail, you try pictures; and where the intellectual perceptions are so dim as to be unable to comprehend pictures, you must have recourse to images. What else is the whole theory of the doll? So that the grosser sense of feeling may, as with a blind man, be the blessed medium between God and the soul. The spiritual world is not so very far removed from the physical. Mental blindness requires as tender treatment as bodily blindness.

"Who would rush at a benighted man,
    And give him two black eyes for being blind?"

asks one who has yet to be recognized as one of the wisest of modern philosophers. And not without reason does poor Hood put the question. For instead of consulting your own natural feelings in your treatment of these heathen, you have rather adopted the temper and imitated the conduct of the Jews of old, as told in their sacred books. Proud of the lofty refinement of your own perceptions of Deity, and unable to imagine yourselves so low down in the scale of intelligence as to think like savages, you denounce them as wilful dishonourers of God, and would destroy, or if you will, "improve them" off the face of the earth, when all the time they may be acting up more nearly to their light than yourselves, or even than the ferocious old Jews whom you so delight to honour.'

'But these worship not God, but devils, and hideous images of devils. They think that the kind being who sends them the gentle breeze and showers, and makes the fruit to grow and the fish to swarm, and causes all their happiness and prosperity,

does not exact costly offerings from them.
These they reserve for the cruel beings
who send the hurricane and the famine, in
order to avert their wrath, and purchase
their forbearance. What is this but devil-
worship ? '

' What indeed ! Well, well. Among
Christians too I have heard something of
a doctrine of propitiation. Among Christians I have heard something of a powerful being who brought all the evil and
misery into the world. Of course people
will pay most attention to that which they
think most powerful to do them good or
harm. I have known even Christian children inquire why, if God was the strongest,
he did not kill the devil, and Christian
mothers were unable to answer the question to their satisfaction. So that it is
little wonder that these poor people seem
to pay most homage where they think they
have most reason to fear.

' "Cannibalism"? A most uncomfortable practice for us even to think of, and one that shows how men crave for animal food. The craving exists. No teaching or denunciation can get rid of that, or of any other propensity. It must be recognized and controlled, and its proper satisfaction provided for. Men's lusts, as you technically term those natural desires, the abuse of which produces the greatest personal demoralization and social inconvenience, are not bad things in themselves. They only require proper means of gratification. Give cannibals good wholesome meat, and they will soon cease to care to eat each other.

' Polygamy one of your greatest difficulties? I can readily believe that this jump from patriarchal habits is too great to be made at once. By insisting on the repudiation of all wives but one, may you not only be doing a cruel injustice to the poor women themselves, but also be confounding European customs with Christian essentials ?

'I do not wonder at your feeling discouraged, but it is somewhat remarkable how you have contrived to keep your reports published at home free from betraying this feeling. You admit that the reality falls far short of the exorbitant ideas there. You say that you are expected to do more in a single generation for these savages than Christianity has done in eighteen centuries for the Europeans. But have you been careful not to excite and foster this unreasonable expectation ?'

'Fault of human nature ! people must be worked up into giving their money ! Besides, what is here but a simple statement about a strange race, may there appear exciting from its very novelty; and it is difficult to make it otherwise.'

' Perhaps. But notwithstanding your theory that earth is but a nursery for heaven, and that your business is only to produce conditions favourable to the saving of souls, it is plain that you suffer the despondency consequent on your conviction that you are striving to elevate a vanishing race. You mark the gradual decline of the population. Why it is, you know not. In these islands at least there is no apparent cause, no disease or fatal habit introduced to account for it. Wherever the white man sets his foot, the aborigine disappears. Like wild beasts disturbed in their lairs, they go away, they cease to breed. The natives are instinctively aware of this. They await their extinction as a thing that sooner or later must happen. And thus they lack the most powerful inducement a people can have to elevate itself,—that of bequeathing a glorious nationality to posterity.'

Such on various occasions was the up-
shot of many chats with the missionaries,
when joining them in their repast of fruit
and cocoa-nut milk, a jug of which, fresh
and cool, is always on the table at meals;
or in accompanying them either on foot
over the hills, or by water in a canoe to
some remote station.

*   *   *   *

Our missionaries object to the Romish
ones that they merely substitute one set of
idols for another, and so give the natives a
religion not essentially differing from their
own.   I think it may be equally objected
to our missionaries that they offer to the
worship of the savages no other deity than
they already recognize, but maintain the
heathen conception of a God who requires
to be propitiated and appeased by sacrifice
and blood.   They thus propagate the
Jewish and Pagan idea of atonements, and

confirm their disciples in their belief in a God who requires the blood of the guilt-less to enable him to pardon the guilty. It is possible that Christianity, or the aboli-tion of the belief in sacrifice, if such be its proper definition, has still all its way to make. That the Church itself is not yet Christian, but Jewish: the Law still in force, and the Gospel a dead letter. If so, the contest will come some day, and will be a severe one when it comes. The vast majority holding to the old idea will fight hard, and the new reformation will doubt-less have its martyrs. I don't see how it can take place *within* the Church of Eng-land. There must be another Exodus.

*   *   *   *

If the above idea be correct, in recom-mending the religion of Christ to the Jews, the Apostles, and especially St Paul, must have gone too far in accommodating it to Jewish prepossessions by representing

his death as a substitute for their sacrifices.
St Paul's language, distinct as it seems to
us, may really have only meant, 'If you
must have a sacrifice and a victim, accept
this as one. You cannot find a nobler and
more unblemished.' He may have said
this to win them over without meaning
that Christ's death really had such a signi-
fication. And if he did mean it, it is not
necessarily a truth for all time.

*　　　*　　　*　　　*

Probably the best effect of our missionaries is the example they afford of domes-
ticity. Content with one wife who lives
on terms of equality with her husband,
and finding happiness in the culture of
their children, they far transcend their
Romish rivals, whose lonely lives seem intended to teach that obedience to the laws
of our being is incompatible with true
holiness. The celibate missionary may

make the best proselytes, but the married one will make the best men and women.

Our missionaries have also done the islanders a great service in reducing their language to writing, and so laying the foundations of a native literature. The language, however, is necessarily limited to the number of objects with which the natives are conversant. The missionaries, therefore, found no words in which to express things strange to them. In translating the New Testament the difficulty was constantly experienced in rendering into Samoan not only the various terms relating to spiritual matters, but the names of animals, and other names familiar elsewhere. Thus, for many years, the only quadruped known on the islands were the pigs left there by the first navigators. 'Pig,' therefore, became the generic term for all animals with four legs. The cow is the 'large lowing milk pig.' The horse is the 'great fast-running pig.' The sheep is the 'hairy pig'—a phrase that proved particularly awkward, when, in translating the Testament, it became necessary to find a Samoan equivalent for ' Lamb of God.' I wonder how many theological dogmas owe their origin to a similar poverty of language.

*   *   *   *

It would be a curious study to trace the variety in language to differences of climate. All warm countries have soft dialects. That of the islands is almost devoid of consonants, witness the names of the Sandwich Islands, Oahoo, Honolulu, Owhyhee; as well as all those of the South Seas. The consonants inserted by the missionaries in writing are hardly detectable in the speech of a native.

They surpass the Italians in their horror of mutes, and barely indicate even the liquid sounds. The guttural tones of the north would seem to have originated in throats rough and voices thick from perpetual colds, when all the north of Europe was marsh and damp forest. What a contrast are the labial languages of the South. Compare Italian with German!

*　　*　　*　　*

It is probable that a little investigation would discover a meaning and a truth under the rites and symbols even of the rudest savages. The hideous Hindoo goddess Kali, all mouths and weapons, girt with human heads and revelling in blood, is, like the Greek Kronos, who devoured his own children, only a poetic personification of Time—' edax rerum.' How much easier would be the task of the missionary were he to try to learn before beginning to teach. To learn the nature of man before dogmatizing about that of God.

*　　*　　*　　*

Methinks there are worse idolaters than these poor savages ever were, even those who cling to their conventional symbols long after they have perceived how utterly they fail to represent the Infinite for them.

CHAPTER VII.

A NEW PASSENGER.

ONE glimpse of the Feejees and we
are off again on our course for Sydney.
No cargo to be got here, as the natives are
busy fighting. They are splendid-looking
fellows, darker and fiercer than the Samoans, and inveterate cannibals. The practice of man-eating must cause them to
regard human nature from a point of view
altogether unknown to us. Probably the
sight of a stranger excites in them much
the same critical feeling that the sight of a
bullock does in the cattle farmer. We

have gained a passenger, a Roman Catholic missionary. He turns out to be an Irishman, though speaking French by preference and habit,—a genial kind of man, and apparently sincere. But this last it is hard to predicate of any one with whom profession has long been a vocation.

The captain, who is shrewd enough, has already established a bantering relationship with the priest.

'Better fun out here than among the bogtrotters at home, aye?' an observation to which the priest, who is contemplating the receding islands, deems a reply unnecessary.

'I suppose,' continues the captain, 'there is as much love of adventure beneath a black coat as any other. And that's the secret of a good many of you missionaries coming to the islands.'

Priest hopes that they have better motives than that, though such an impulse may be used as instrument of good.

Captain 'hopes no offence, but doesn't see what good it can do to make the savages worship a bit of bread instead of a bit of wood.'

'Perhaps you have never tried to see it,' is the mild response.

'My glass hasn't got a lens strong enough,' rejoins the captain.

Then as you admit you do not understand these matters, you will do me a great favour by not speaking irreverently of them.'

'However, I think I can see as far as most men with the naked eye, though I haven't got a patent magnifier,' persisted the captain. 'But I should like to know more about the bit of bread. I can understand a man believing that everything is only part of God, for I have heard the Brahmins in the East Indies argue with our missionaries that, though a drop of water can't float a ship, yet the ocean is made up of drops, and that in the same way all things together make up God. But what puzzles me is why you Catholics should pick out bread as being God, and leave out other things.'

'You are a sailor, and should know what " obeying orders " means.'

'To be sure, when a man hears them given by his captain.'

'Or when they come from the captain through any superior officer.'

'I see what you are driving at, but it's not quite such plain sailing when you come to matters of priestcraft.'

'Have you ever heard of such a thing as faith ? '

'Many a time, but I prefer experience.'

'Nay, have you ever been in these seas before ? '

'Never.'

'Then what guide have you to keep you clear of reefs?'

'I've got the best Admiralty charts, and my own eyes into the bargain.'

'You have had no experience of these latitudes or of the charts describing them, and yet you venture your very life upon them. What is this but faith?'

'Let me ask a question too? You know nothing about the seaworthiness of this craft, or the ability of her master. Why, you might have come aboard a regular pirate for anything you know. When I come to think of it I quite wonder at your rashness.'

'Oh, with regard to that,' said the priest laughing, 'I saw you had got safe so far, and so must be a pretty good sailor. And I have seen too many vessels not to know when they are all right.'

'There now,' exclaimed the captain, in

a tone of mock disappointment, 'I was going to give you credit for faith, and I find it's only experience after all.'

The priest bit his lip on seeing the trap he had fallen into, but asked quietly, 'Do you make any account of other men's experience, or use your own only?'

'Oh, I use all I can get that seems dependable.'

'But what enables you to decide what is dependable? Things may have happened to other people quite different from anything you have seen.'

'I judge if they are dependable in other respects, and if what they say is natural and likely, and whether they have any interest in deceiving me.'

'And you regard as false all testimony to events which pass ordinary comprehension?'

'I only say that I judge by experience.'

'But the events to which I allude, though they contradict your experience, did not contradict that of others.'

'Those who saw them have a right to believe them. But that is just what you want people not to do, when you say a bit of bread is changed into God; when all the time neither I nor anybody else can see a particle of difference in it.'

Baffled a second time, the priest took advantage of some interruption to allow the discussion to drop, and it occurred to me that no amount of reasoning will do any good in opening the popular mind, until the true history of Christianity is written, exhibiting the utter absence of anything like real evidence to justify the popular belief. Even then, until far enough advanced to recognize the Divine in the grand harmony and invariable order of nature, people will only believe that those particular interruptions did not take place;

not that all interruption is impossible.

I don't want to get engaged in these controversies. The priest has a good deal of interesting information on other subjects connected with these seas. Anybody who wants to know about the islands should read this book of Melville's, 'Typee,' which the captain has just lent me. How vivid are his descriptions. His 'Fayaway' must have been something like my poor Maleia. He completely carries me back to the island.

I suspect that if the truth were known of the conduct of white sailors in the Pacific islands, we should not wonder so much at the barbarous massacres that sometimes take place. The natives must have come to look upon white men as fiends. One story of a whaler I must make a note of. The priest says he got it from one of the men concerned, and is firmly convinced of its truth :—

'In the year 1827, there were three men

named Brag, and three named Bully, all masters of vessels trading in the South Seas, and all insufferable tyrants.

'One of the Brags once took it into his head that the ship's cook had the scurvy, or the sulks, and buried him up to his neck in the ship's ballast. While there, he flung a crowbar at his head and killed him. He then gave out a supply of rum to the crew, and when all hands were drunk made them sign a certificate that the cook had died a natural death, and put the paper carefully by. On reaching home the men gave information of the murder, and the master was tried for it. His counsel asserted that the accusation was the result of a conspiracy on the part of the crew against their captain, and produced the paper with their own signatures in proof. Whereupon he was acquitted. The end of this man was a fitting one. When offended with his crew on one occasion, he swore that as soon as he reached New Zealand he would have them roasted and eaten. Such was his disposition and his influence with the chiefs, that they were terrified at the threat, and determined to get rid of him. So, one morning when the vessel was slowly drawing through the water, the crew agreed to throw him overboard. The majority were mending sails forward, and the captain sat by the taffrail, also sewing. The cook's going to the cabin to take away breakfast was the signal. Some of the men gathered as if unconcernedly about the captain. Others pinioned the mate, and the captain was in a moment thrown overboard. He swam after the ship entreating to be taken in. Sometimes he could just touch the rudder, and then he would be a few yards astern again; and so he was for many minutes, begging to be taken on board. They only replied by throwing over to him an empty cask,

which turned over and over as he attempted to get upon it, and served merely
to prolong his efforts, until he was at last
drowned.'

CHAPTER VIII.

NOTCHES.

CONTRARY to my wish I have had a brief passage at arms with the priest. A general conversation about the islands led him to remark that the belief in the divine origin of sacrifice received confirmation even among cannibals, for it illustrated the Church's maxim, ' Quod semper, ubique, et ab omnibus.'

I replied, that not only was the maxim incapable of verification, but that even if any belief could be shown to have been universal among primitive tribes, it would prove nothing. That as for the doctrine of sacrifice, it was gradually losing its hold upon the human mind, the whole Protestant world regarding it as having been accomplished once for all; while there are indications that the most thinking minds of our own age are abandoning the idea altogether as a human figment. And that if universal consent could prove anything, it would prove that the sun goes round the earth.

Hereupon the captain rubbed his hands, and declared he should hand his Reverence over to me for the rest of the voyage.

Without noticing this speech, the priest replied, gently, that he had little sympathy with the modern tendency to shift religious faith from its eternal foundations to square with any scientific theory that happened to be uppermost. Faith should be the same yesterday, to-day, and for ever, quite regardless of the changes in human opinions about things.

I observed that for my part I could not recognize the necessity of any antagonism between Faith and Fact. That where my choice lay between what other men told me to believe, and my own perceptions, I preferred the latter.

He said that if by the phrase 'other men' I meant the Church, he denied that it was a fair equivalent.

And then I changed the subject, not wishing, though I hardly know why, to establish an habitual controversy with him. It seems to me scarcely fair to argue about what is not an open question for my opponent. All questions are open for me. I am free to follow truth wherever it may lead me, without fear or loss. But it is not so with him. As the little Frenchman said once, he gets his bread by teaching the opinions of his sect. If I convert him,

he will either starve, or continue to teach
what he has ceased to believe. And I do
not wish to be responsible for his doing
either. I believe, however, that my reluct-
ance arises from a doubt of his sincerity.
With any one who is really anxious to find
the truth I should be most delighted to talk;
but not with those who desire merely to
maintain a foregone conclusion.

I have been greatly amused by hearing the Frenchman defending the priest
against the captain, and at the same time
covertly attacking the side he had himself
espoused. It is the first time he has taken
any part in these sparring matches which
the captain so delights to commence. We
were all on the poop. I was reading, the
Frenchman was fixing a bait for a shark
that was following the vessel as she slowly
drew through the smooth water, and the
other two were talking about I know not
what; but the captain was in his usual

bantering humour, when the Frenchman exclaimed,

'And pray how do you know it is not true?'

'Why,' said the captain, 'because it directly contradicts what I do know to be true.'

'Is that a reason? Do you see that monster? Is not he true? Am not I true? And do we agree together? No! no! When I see a shark, or a tiger, or a snake, or a mosquito, I say to them, "You are divine, for you are made by the same Being that made me, and everything. We are all of us *manifestations* of a divine idea; but we do not agree. I will either kill you, or I will get out of your way." And so I say to the dogma of the priests: "I do not deny that you are divine and true, but I and my opinion are so also; and as we do not agree, I will have nothing to say to you, but will leave you alone. You may be good friends with the other monsters, but if you come troubling me I will try to destroy you." Aha! aha! he does bite, now monsieur shark, you are one true shark, and you will find dat is one true hook, and I am one true Frenchman, but we shall not agree very well with you, I do think.'

And so the materials for my note terminate in the excitement of the capture.

*   *   *   *

The very existence of such horrid brutes certainly makes it very hard to believe in any doctrine of final causes. If sharks, why not devils?

Frenchman says,

'Ah, why not? it is only a question of evidence.' 'Poor brutes,' he added, 'give a man as little to eat in proportion to his appetite, and you will make a devil or a shark of him.'

*　　*　　*　　*

Of a future life he says, ' It may be, but there are immense difficulties in the way.'

*　　*　　*　　*

I suspect the little Frenchman is a better philosopher than I am. His mind is purely inductive. He does not even assume a theory to enable him to classify his facts. Whereas I am for ever deducing a theory from a rapid survey of facts, and then analyzing them to see how far they verify my theory. Yet to have no theory is to be rather empirical than inductive. Probably the particular question just referred to is one of definition rather than of theory. What is meant by a ' devil'? A being entirely at variance with the laws of its Creator. But those laws impose the conditions of its being. In utter violation of those conditions it cannot continue to exist. Unmitigated evil, it has been said, must destroy itself. A devil then is that which by our very definition of it cannot exist. If it exists it must be some other kind of being, namely, one that does not altogether oppose God's laws. Then it is no devil, and my instinctive disbelief in such a creature is founded in truth. Perhaps this verdict was intended as a compromise between impossibility and orthodoxy—'the devil is not so black as he is painted.'

*   *   *   *

The belief in the necessity of sacrificing to the Deity seems to be the earliest form taken by that fear of the Unknown which we call superstition. It is probably founded both on the difficulty man finds in forgiving or foregoing his own revenge without some compensation or equivalent, and on his own aptness for being propitiated by gifts.

'The popular theory of Christianity is singularly illogical. If mercy and forgiveness be virtues, it entirely deprives the Deity of the merit of possessing them. If the debt be paid there is no room for forgiveness. So long as the creditor gets his money it is nothing to him where it comes from.

'But in this consists the mercy of God. He himself pays the penalty for our transgression.'

'That is, it is not paid at all. It is only as if I transferred my money from one of my pockets to another.'

'It is profane to reason concerning a mystery which faith alone can comprehend.'

'Yet you hold it up to my admiration! No, no, I must first exercise my reason upon it in order to ascertain that it is a matter which requires to be referred to the category of faith.' Theologians always appeal to faith when reason fails them. They do not, however, fail to employ reason so long as it is on their own side. I wonder what state of things I shall find in Australia. The priest's account agrees with what the other missionaries told me, that religious faction ran high before the gold discovery.

*　　*　　*　　*

Yonder curious outlines, one peak and two hummocks, bearing north-west about twenty miles off, are Ball's pyramid and Lord Howes' Island. How it has blown for the last ten days! Most of the time we have been lying to, with heavy seas breaking over the ship, making it impossible to cook anything.

There is something about the priest that I like much. He has stuck to his rubber with the rest of us through the whole of the hurricane. Certainly whist is a capital pastime at sea, requiring no additional excitement of gambling.

What an odd spectacle for a landsman filled with the traditional terrors of the sea, would be this fragile wooden vessel, banged furiously about by the huge waves, lying now on one side, now on the other, now plunging head foremost into the trough of the sea as if on the point of being irrevocably overwhelmed, and now actually submerged beneath the broken waters which rush in a torrent over the decks, and in a little compartment, four men quietly engaged in a game at cards, dealing with one hand and holding on with the other, quite regardless of the dreadful pother of the elements without.

—A spectacle not unyielding of a moral. Horace's ode ' Integer vitæ, scelerisque purus,' may be rendered in sailor phraseology, ' Make all snug within, and let the gale blow itself out.'

*   *   *   *

It is curious to see how void of all

conception of what we English call 'duty,'
the little Frenchman is. I was talking
with him about the opposition and en-
mity incurred by those who, having perceived new truths, endeavour to perform
their duty in promulgating them. He
observed that he could recognize no such
obligation. People who discover a truth
may be led by a generous impulse to pub-
lish it, in the hope of doing away with
some evil caused by a falsehood; but their
benevolence will generally meet with ingratitude on the part of those whom they
would benefit. He believes that ulti-
mately the publication of truth will do
good, that is, make mankind happier.
But its first and immediate effect is to
create confusion and dismay. The benevolent theorist finds his reward in contemplating the future. If men are honestly
impelled to submit to martyrdom, they
doubtless find their compensation in their

satisfaction at having obeyed the true impulses of their nature.

As for disturbing the popular faith of
a country, he thinks it quite impossible
to say that it ought or ought not to be
done. When the man appears who is
capable and eager to make a revolution,
he will do so, and quite as grave a respon-
sibility rests upon those who resist the in-
novation, as upon him who makes it. They
indeed may resist, and generally do resist,
from mere indolent habit; but he comes
with what may be new light from the
eternal source, for he has not got it from
them. Until proved wrong he is a prophet, and the bitterest antagonist of the
prophet is the priest.

'You know of course,' I said, laughing,
'where our orthodox folks would say he
and his light came from?'

'Ah, no, there is only one source for
everything.'

'You forget the devil—'

'Ah, I do beg his pardon. I forgot the Christian's bad god. Satan is his name, I remember, now.'

He added this caution,—

'You are eager to open people's eyes and to show them what you have seen yourself. Mark me, people do not want to have their eyes opened, not in Australia, nor in Europe. They are accustomed to a certain light, and they have come to like it. If you go against their priests, you who tell me you belong to a clergyman's family, they will attack you as a traitor to their order, who, after being initiated into their secrets, turns round upon them and exposes them. Think how *enragés* would be the priests of any religion, if one of their number published to the world that their sacred books, which they had taught men to believe to come from the gods and be infallible, were written

by men and full of mistakes and contra-
dictions! If you are so benevolent that
you must speak out, try to wait till you
are in a safe position where nobody can
make you starve. Besides, they will be
more likely to believe a man when he has
five thousand pounds *rente*. You do not
belong to a free country where a man can
speak out a strange opinion and not suffer.
Your English people are great bigots.
They are ignorant of all things outside of
themselves, and ignorant people are always
bigots, for they do not know how little
they know, but think that little is everything. You may have to go to Paris for a
wife, unless you pay great respects to
English prejudices.'

Serious threats these, starvation and
a French wife! The first I have tried
and did not like at all. The second
would equally disagree with me, if my
idea of French women be correct.

* * * *

The Frenchman says, 'God has given us infallibility in nothing except mathematics.' Can it be said that we have it there, when feeling is the only basis of demonstration ?

He says, he 'does not see why we should expect perfection in the world. It may be one of the earliest attempts at creation, and only practice can make perfect.'

He gives a new reason for the celibacy of the clergy. 'The Church must sooner or later fall when the priests have families who know as much about the system as the priests themselves know, and have not the same interest in maintaining it.'

Talking of the Americans, he said that France is freest socially, England politically, and America religiously. England and France have much to learn from each other, and some day will learn it. But he

does not believe in the Americans. 'Their
civilization is not real, springing from the
character of the people themselves; it is
merely remembered, or imitative. They
have no notion of discipline, and he
wouldn't be surprised at anything that
may happen to them. Whenever a serious
crisis or convulsion comes, the lawyers will
have it all their own way; and woe betide
a people governed by lawyers, for they
have no sense of right and justice in the
abstract, but only in relation to the statute
book. A thing is made right and proper
for them by being enacted by authority.
So that when they do get the upper hand
they will enact anything to suit their own
purposes; and it will take soldiers to put
down the lawyers. So attorney-like is the
nation's mind that the people themselves
generally hold that a good lie, well stuck
to, is better than the truth. A man by

telling the truth exposes his game and puts himself at a disadvantage.'

I remarked that I had certainly heard it said that truth is too sacred a thing to be used except on emergencies, but that of course was in joke. But with reference to slavery it seemed clear to me that the negroes had a terrible revenge for their oppression, for that whatever of national degeneration the Americans were suffering, they owed it to the influences of slavery.

Frenchman said he was not quite so sure of that. He knows the States well, and the only gentlemen are the planters. The Northerners are all politically cowards, as all traders are, afraid to have any opinions of their own, or to express them if they have. A Frenchman or Englishman does not care if he stands alone in his opinion, he will utter it in defiance of the

whole world. But a Yankee depends on
the public opinion of his party. He does
not believe he is right unless recognized
by newspapers.

I said I had heard more than one
Southerner express admiration of Louis
Napoleon, and wish for a despotic government in America; but I thought that
a slave-owner, though he might like to
be absolute over his slaves, would scarcely
like a despot over himself.

'Quite the contrary,' said the Frenchman, 'a strong government would be a
new sensation for many Americans, and
they would delight in it, especially if it
released them from the popular tyranny
they have now. The respectable classes
would then be in a better position.'

But this strikes me as a peculiarly
shrewd remark: 'that with a mixed race a
republic is an impossibility unless one be

dominant. The blacks, if free, must have their share in the government. The whites cannot suffer this. Wherefore, the total abolition of slavery and of political inequality will lead to the destruction of the republic and the substitution of a despotism. For a single race a representative government is best; for a mixed population it is impossible. Autocracy, or slavery.'

BOOK VI.

16

'Friendship requires that rare mean betwixt likeness and unlikeness, that piques each with the presence of power and of consent in the other party. Let me be alone to the end of the world rather than that my friend should overstep by a word or by a look his real sympathy. I am equally baulked by antagonism and by compliance. Let him not cease for an instant to be himself. The only joy I have in his being mine is that the not mine is mine.'—R. W. EMERSON's 'Friendship.'

> 'But thou and I are one in kind,
>   As moulded like in nature's mint;
>   And hill and wood and field did print
> The same sweet forms in either mind.'
>   TENNYSON's 'In Memoriam.'

CHAPTER I.

THE ANTIPODES.

To Charles Arnold.

Sydney.

DEAR FRIEND,

I have delayed writing to you until
my plans and ideas should have time to
take some definite form.

You cannot think what a treat it is to
be among one's own countrymen again.
Everything is so English. The colonists
have reproduced the old home so exactly
that I felt on first walking through Sydney as if I could have turned up any
street and gone home in a few minutes.

There were such fearful accounts in San Francisco of the anarchy and violence prevailing here, that it was matter of serious discussion before our arrival whether we should go ashore armed. The others were in favour of doing so, but I said, 'No, no, we are going among our own countrymen, and I for one will not distrust them until forced to do so,' and the pilot laughed them out of the notion before landing. As far as I can now judge, there is not a more peaceable population in the world.

Coming here a total stranger and without a single introduction, I was most fortunate in lighting upon some friends and even connections of my family, and so placed as to give me the opportunity of seeing the people and the country to the best advantage. The hospitality I meet with is doubly grateful after all my wanderings and privations. Just now I am staying in a house that stands on an eminence overlooking the harbour. The mornings I am at present devoting to reading or writing; but half the time is lost in looking out of the window—yet not lost, the prospect is so lovely. It is worth a voyage round the world to see this Sydney bay. The deep blue of the water, fringed with the innumerable indentations of a shore rising abruptly from it and covered with vegetation, with here and there beautiful little islets, paradises for picnics, and, over all, the soft dreamy haze we used to admire so in Finden's views of the American lakes, with white sails moving about in all directions, form altogether a scene of such enchanting beauty, as to move one even to tears when alone and gazing on it. Why such should be the effect of surpassing beauty in a landscape, I know not. But I have always found a feeling of profound melancholy come over me at such a time. The melancholy being always proportionate to the sense of beauty, when the beauty is soft and harmonious, not rugged and sublime.

Does the conviction that there is infinitely more beauty than one can appreciate produce mortification at our inability to grasp the whole—a 'divine despair' at our own incapacity? Or is it that the brain becomes so acutely impressed as to require the relief of tears, its tension producing a fever of which tears are the relieving perspiration? But this only accounts for the tears, not for the melancholy. That, I take it, arises from a sense of unsatisfied desire—unsatisfied although filled to overflowing, inasmuch as all beauty is most beautiful when most suggestive of something more than, something beyond, beauty; as a human face is fairest when it indicates most lovable qualities.

I have seen faces of which I could not

but admire the form of the features and the complexion, but though possessing all the external qualifications for beauty, they were not beautiful, for they were no index to beauty of soul lying beneath. It is no beauty that is only skin-deep; for true beauty is no external accident, but a revelation of that which is within. Yet if the eye can only see that which it has the power of seeing, the beauty of the object will vary with the perception of the beholder. Like taste and smell, it does not exist in the object, but is the result or sensation caused by combination or contact with one's own faculty of perception:—an effect, not a quality. The feeling for beauty must be an indication of a certain amount of moral vigour. To be dead to that is to be dead to all things. They are not wholly dead to whom Persius applies that remarkable line :—

  '*Virtutem videant, intabescantque relictâ.*'

But you will be retorting my Latin upon me, and saying, 'Cœlum non animum mutat.'

The Sunday after my arrival, I, for the first time since leaving England, went to church. It was so curious: just like being metamorphosed backwards into a previous state of existence. Everything was exactly what I have been accustomed to at home. The women in their smartest silks rustling into their little rectangular boxes of pews:—the men in what a backwoodsman would call their 'Sunday-go-to-meeting trowserloons,' putting their faces into the hats out of which they had just taken their heads ; the flutter of leaves, the murmur of responses, the glib routine assent to incomprehensible dogmas ; the rapid transitions from the utterances of sorrow and contrition to those of joy and praise, and back again ; the sitting, standing, and kneeling, everything was so ab-

surdly identical that I felt myself expand-
ing into an all-pervading smile at the
ludicrous accuracy of the imitation. Much
as one might be supposed to do if in after
life one could witness one's own juvenile
self enacting the vagaries of one's own
childhood, but without the childish feeling
to prompt them. Being one of the principal churches in Sydney, it was not unnatural to look for some degree of intelligence in the preaching department. It
was thoughtless of me, I own, but until I
heard that sermon I had failed to realize
the vastness of the gulf that separates me
from my former self, and from my kindred
generally. That simple utterance of woe,
' I shall go to him, but he shall not return
to me,' the preacher—a pleasant though
delicate and sentimental-looking young
fellow — told us incontrovertibly established the existence of a future life, and
David's belief in it. It proved also that

our faculties of recognizing those whom
we had loved and lost on earth will be
greatly increased there. 'For David evidently looked forward with pleasure to
seeing his child in heaven ; but the changes
that would be made in its appearance by
its translation from the royal nursery to
the society of glorified angels, would prevent his recognizing it unless his faculties
were greatly improved; especially as old
men do not generally take notice of in-
fants so as to know them apart.' I assure
you, upon my honour, that this is, as
nearly as I can remember it, word for
word what the preacher said.   And when
on coming out of church I looked round
among the congregation for expressions of
indignation at his daring to talk such nonsense to grown-up men and women, I
actually saw people turn up their eyes and
exclaim, 'What a lovely discourse!' So
that it seems to have been good enough

for them. For myself I shall not trust myself to go again. It does me harm.

In the pew with me was a young lady who, when the service had been going on for some time, perceived my lack of a prayer-book, and lent me one; but after several vain attempts to find the places I laid it down. The air of mingled wonderment and amusement with which she regarded me showed that she took me for a sort of white savage. But seeing, I suppose, that I did not look dangerous, she very good-naturedly found all the places for me. Her veil prevented me from seeing her face very distinctly, but from the tall graceful figure, and the rich auburn hair lying on the back of the neck, and, above all, the voice when joining in the singing, a voice so rich and full of feeling, and, rarest of all qualities, so capable of making others feel, convince me that she must be both beautiful and good. Her manner, when finding the places for me, was almost motherly, indicating no self-consciousness, but only anxiety to do a service. But, whether beautiful or not, I must own that her presence diffused a sort of charm around, which you will doubtless ascribe to the fact that I am an uncivilized gold-digger, and she *a* woman, (though by no means necessarily *the* woman).

During the sermon I detected myself indignantly uttering the word ' stuff.' I did not know I had done so audibly until I saw her start and look towards me, as if roused from a reverie. She then seemed to listen for a few moments, when I am almost certain I heard her say to herself, ' Why, so it is.'

I had no idea of the amazing power of early associations until I found myself so strangely affected at first by everything that reminded me of the old home. People coming here direct from England note rather the difference than the likeness. But for me, habituated to Spanish, American, and South Sea characteristics, everything human is very English. I can understand now how the mind, in times of great weakness and depression, finds intense comfort in recurring to the convictions of childhood, especially after a life spent at variance with the feelings then instilled ; and how, indeed, it cannot help flying back to them with a force proportioned to the barrenness and neglect of the intervening period,—just as the effect of atmospheric pressure outside a hollow sphere depends upon the completeness of the vacuum within. Not in those cases where early principles have been deliberately and with intellectual labour exchanged for, or developed into, higher and truer perceptions of the nature of things, do we find the notions of the nursery and schoolroom recurring with such overwhelming power as to destroy all that has been gained in after life; unless, indeed, disease has come to obliterate the later acquisitions of the intellect, sparing only the memory of the earliest and most deeply impressed.

But in cases where the early principles have been overlooked in the extravagance of a mere animal existence, the exhaustion of animal vigour leaves the field clear for the return to power of the old habits of feeling and thinking. Poor dying old Falstaff, ' babbling of green fields,' strikes me as one of the truest touches of nature in all Shakspeare. It is ignorance of this natural law that leads people to marvel at the rapid alternations of piety and recklessness to which men of strong, uncontrolled passions sometimes give way; and to exult over the death-bed return of the prodigal to the sentiments of his youth, as a confirmation of the dogmas he has been taught.

It is not at such a time, when in exhaustion, agony, or terror, that the judgment is fittest to decide what is truth ; and
I sometimes think that I shall leave a
written memorandum to the effect that, if
ever I am found to have returned to the
old paths of my early religious sentiments,
it will probably be found that my brain
has given way, and become no longer able
to retain any impressions but those of childhood : so that no physical weakness of
mine may afford a triumph to the enemies
of free thought.

You will be thinking that this is a far-
fetched disquisition to be led into by so
simple a matter as the resemblance of
things in Sydney to things in England.
But the whole tendency of my speculations
for some time past has been to trace
the connection between things apparently
remote from each other, in the belief
that all things are but links in the same

chain or steps in the same process, only some are farther advanced than others; so that the most complicated phenomena may be referred back to causes at once simple and related to each other. The more I am able to see into the nature of the things with which we have to do, whether moral or physical, the more evident does it become to me that the advance of knowledge consists, not in the multiplication of agencies, but in their reduction to unity. I believe that the whole system of psychology and morality is truly deducible from the one governing law of our nature, Selfishness,—a word that may be used in a good, as well as in a bad sense. With his own consciousness for centre, and the Indefinite for distance, it is for man to describe a circle of knowledge ever increasing with his own experiences.

In the great cause of Experience *versus*

Authority, judgment, with costs, is given against the latter; and I find myself no longer harassed by the perplexities incidental to the theory of a revelation external to, and irrespective of, my own perceptions, inasmuch as it is self-evident that it requires a prior knowledge of the Absolute in order to be able to predicate of any information that it is thence immediately derived. When we have said that God is the moving force or life of things, we have said all that we can possibly know or imagine of Him; and this is only a definition or repetition of terms. All real knowledge is not of Him, but of His Method: so inevitably and utterly is the Absolute beyond the reach of all limited beings, that it may be said that for us there is no Absolute; for by the Absolute we can only mean that which is finished and perfect. Whereas the God of our comprehension never rested, never rests, from his work; nor will he do so until nature ceases, and annihilation prevails.

Our experience can be only of the Finite, which cannot in any way represent the Infinite. If man was made in the image of God, surely he has returned the compliment, and made God in the image of himself, endowing Him with all the faculties he himself deems best and greatest. The God of all ages, peoples, and individuals, varies with the stage of their progress in knowledge, and will ever continue to do so; becoming more elevated and refined in the conception of men until they reach that point when they can bow in reverence to the Inscrutable, and own that the theology of every age is but the product and measure of man's knowledge of himself.

The interest you have ever taken in my mental pilgrimage has thus led me to tell

you more about my thoughts than about
the country or my plans in it. My next
letter shall be after I have been into the
interior, and, I hope, got to work at
something; for my holiday has now lasted
several months, and independently of
money reasons, I really long to be at work
again. Having escaped from the Samoan
Capua, I must not make another one of this
pleasant place.

One thing I want you to do for me, and
that is to tell me the names of any good
books on the subjects which occupy me;
not volumes of hearsays, the shops here are
abundantly supplied with them, but men's
own experience in the domains of life.
Humboldt's 'Cosmos' I am now reading.
It is a grand collection of physical facts;
but I want to see the facts classified, and
the process of evolution of the moral from
the physical life traced,—books which help
one to comprehend the vast harmony and

tendency of the universe. From what my little French friend said of Comte's *Philosophie Positive,* it seems to be one of the books I should read.

CHAPTER II.

THE COLONY.

To Charles Arnold.

INNUMERABLE thanks, dear friend, for
the letter and the books. It is a glorious
selection, and exactly what I wanted. I
had no idea that such books existed.
Surely they betoken a vast revolution of
opinion in England ;—nothing less than
the advent of an age of free thought, de-
livered from the tyranny of foregone conclusions, and unfettered by aught but love
of truth. It is intensely pleasant to find
other minds, starting from different points
and travelling by different paths, approach

the same conclusions that I myself, by simply thinking and feeling, have reached. I have as yet only glanced at most of the volumes, reserving the regular reading of them until I can find time; and as I read I shall not fail to bear in mind your caution, and endeavour to ascertain what element there is in human nature which they omit from their account. At present I confess myself at a loss to discern it. I am unable to admit the existence of a spiritual element altogether external to, and independent of, the material, because I do not know the limits or functions of the latter. Once granted the faculty of thought or consciousness, and I do not see what more is wanted to account for all human phenomena, even including the existence of moral evil.

Your argument from the existence of the imagination is certainly one to be kept in mind. It is only the narrowest feeling that would prohibit the use, for fear of the abuse, of anything. To ignore the proper functions of the imagination lest it betray us into superstition, is only to fall into the same error as the religionist who through dread of scepticism ignores his reason. But if by the imagination you mean some transcendental faculty capable of acquiring knowledge independently of experience, it seems to me that you are at once assuming the whole question and deposing reason from the exercise of any office whatever. For whatever conclusions reason may come to, they must all be abandoned at the bidding of the imagination; whereas it seems to me that the latter should be the handmaid and co-adjutor of the reason, not its supplanter. But surely all these complications are only the result of a vicious metaphysics. The reason and the imagination are, after all, but modes of thought, and it is a very defective capacity that can only think in one way.

I have come across one book in this country that seems to contain the root of all possible thought on these subjects. As it was by a somewhat singular chance, I shall give it to you in its proper place in the narrative of my colonial experiences. The months since my last letter, have seen me, first a gold-digger for some months; till I knocked up with the heat, having gained little beside getting thoroughly *en rapport* with the country : the hard work taking off all sense of strangeness, and completely naturalizing me to Australia. The mines much resemble those of California, but are less convenient for working, owing to the irregularity of the water supply. Since that, I have become a government official, holding a post connected with the mines, and in that capacity I have to travel often between them and Sydney. I undertook the post in compliance with the urgent advice of my friends, who assured me I should lose all I have if I trusted to my own resources. I suspect, however, though I don't tell them so, that certain old-country notions about manual labour being ' un-respectable ' had a good deal to do with the advice.

Mounted, and on the road with a couple of hundred miles of mountain and forest, or, as it is called here, ' Bush,' before me, I could fancy myself back in America again. But the illusion is soon dispelled by the difference of the foliage. After the solemn magnificence of the pine-forest, these dingy untidy gum-trees, with leaves so small and scanty as to produce no shade, have a very dismal aspect. But for all that, the country has a capacity which the colonists have not been slow to take advantage of. Now and then one comes to an open plain with fields and farms and cheerful habitations, looking all the more charming for their contrast with the surrounding wilderness of gum-trees. Thus, at the end of the first day's ride from Sydney, the Nepean river breaks from a barrier of tremendous sand-stone cliffs, and winds through the beautiful vale of Mulgoa, with its rich meadow-lands, vineyards, orangeries, and gardens of fruits and flowers enclosing really handsome dwellings :—a very oasis lying at the foot of the Blue Mountains, and which I always contrive to make my stopping place, having been so fortunate as to meet some of the proprietors of this paradise in Sydney. And their hospitality is conferred with such kindliness, as to make it appear that they are the favoured party.

On one of my journeys I thought I knew the country well enough to take a short cut through the bush, and got lost. After passing the night among the gum-trees, I and my horse were travelling on exceedingly famished and uncomfortable, knowing only that our general direction was eastwards. Meeting a shepherd, I learnt that I was very far from everywhere except the head station of his master, whose name I knew as that of one of the principal settlers in that district. Towards this I bent my way, and after some miles came to a fine, open, undulating country, with fields and cottages, and a handsome stone house standing apart. The whole having such an aspect of comfort and refinement, that, hungry as I was, I sought a hidden place on the river that skirted the plain, and took a bath before presenting myself at the house. On introducing myself, the proprietor, a pleasant elderly gentleman, at once asked me in to join him at break-fast, and called a man to take my horse to the stable. We chatted away and soon be-came good friends. He seemed as much pleased to have a visitor as I was with my own good fortune, and evidently enjoyed the glances that, in spite of my eager appetite, I could not help casting at the drawings on the walls, and the delicately worked ornaments of the room. The whole had an aspect so different from anything I had before seen in the far bush-land. Not merely a refined and feminine aspect, but indicating such supreme good taste and high breeding. Everything was good. I suppose I must have looked occasionally towards the door, as if expecting some one else, for my host remarked that although there was no one but himself to entertain me, he hoped I would not think of going before next day. So I stayed, and learnt that he had long been a widower with an only daughter, who had lived there until the gold discovery; that he had ceased to live there now, but came occasionally to visit the station.

He was evidently filled with a sense of
his daughter's perfections, for he delighted
in showing her handiwork and in hearing
my expressions of approbation, which were
really warm and unfeigned, and quite won
his heart, for he took me into his own
room and showed me triumphantly a portrait of a fair young girl of exceeding love-
liness, whom he called his sunbeam, until
I fancied that even I felt a sweet influence
pervading the whole dwelling. Nor was
the fancy dispelled when we went out into
her flower-garden, or when in passing near
the cottages ('huts' they are called here),
the women came out and asked with evident affection after 'Miss Mary.' But this
is a long story, with no other object than
to introduce the book of which I spoke,
and which I found in the library, and,
being attracted by the title, looked over.
It was D'Holbach's 'Système de la Nature,' a book as old as the French Revolu-

tion, and yet laying the foundation for all
future thought, as far as I can foresee its
probable course. A curious book to light
upon in the bush, where the chief cost of
everything is its carriage. Seeing how I
was attracted by it my host said I must
return some day and finish it. He gave
me his address near Sydney, where his
daughter is living together with an invalid
aunt. So that I may yet see the original
of the portrait.

I was prepared to find Australian institutions much like those of England; but
I was rather astonished on discovering that
the colonists so dearly cherish the connection between Church and State, as to have
no less than four State-paid religions, consisting of the most numerous sects, including the Roman Catholic. Of course
there are many who are dissatisfied with
this arrangement; but these are said generally to belong to some of the unrecognized

sects, who get none of the money. 'Endow all or none,' is their demand. Yet,
absurd as the present arrangement may
appear, is it not less so than that assump-
tion of infallibility by which a government
considers itself justified in selecting some
one set of rites and opinions, and taxing the
whole community to support them ? Here,
indeed, the government does not pretend
to pronounce which is the true faith; but
accepting success as the most tangible
test, it subsidizes the clergy of the largest
denominations as a sort of theological po-
lice, necessary to the preservation of social
order; and they, so long as they get the
money, are content to be in this position.

The more I see of the contrast between
the American system and ours, the more I
admire the simplicity of the former. Theirs,
being founded upon first principles, is in
fact a recognition of an universal truth and
justice, existing independently of shifting

policy. Ours, on the contrary, is a deification of the most miserable short-sighted expediency. We take possession of a wilderness, and forthwith transfer to it governors, and bishops, and all the weighty encumbrances of the Old World; and when the emigrant seeks a fresher air and soil, and simpler conditions of existence, he finds himself still confined and fettered by the tangled growth of by-gone ages.

I can anticipate your defence of the institutions I am finding fault with. You will say that men will be apt to leave perfect ones to work themselves, and so neglect the duties, and lose the virtues, of citizens: while the consciousness of imperfection in the system, and therefore of the necessity of care in its administration to prevent a dead-lock, induces moderation and forbearance among different classes: that experience is the only test, and that when a thing is found to work well in

practice no amount of theory ought to
weigh against it.   We have talked of these
matters in the olden time, and while now,
as then, I partly agree, I see more clearly
than ever that, in order to maintain the
less perfect forms of society, it is necessary
to mix with education a certain amount of
prejudice to make the individual fit for the
system.   But however this may be, it is no
matter of wonder to me that the colonial
government is involved in numerous perplexities through its usurpation of functions
which do not properly belong to it.   I was
in the legislative council one day during
the passing of the estimates.   The annual
grant for orphan asylums caused a good
deal of discussion, as well it might, for the
government is committed to the support of
two,—one for Protestant and the other for
Roman Catholic orphans!   The next item
was for the lunatic asylum, when I shocked
my neighbour by inquiring if there were

274 THE PILGRIM AND THE SHRINE.

not two,—one for the Protestant and the
other for Roman Catholic lunatics. I am
convinced by what I see here that the support of religion and charity by the State
has a necessary tendency to destroy them
among the people. Even if the contrary
were the case, the government would not
be justified in undertaking these offices, for
it seems to me incontestable that the true
purpose of a State is, not to promote *directly*
the moral or physical good of society, but
to secure the greatest possible liberty for
every one to do as he pleases;—to follow
religion, wealth, amusement, or anything
else; the sole limitation to his liberty being
the equal liberty of everybody else. No
doubt such freedom will conduce to the
highest good of which society is capable;
not to believe this is the most palpable
Atheism:—but whether it does or not, is
no business of the government. There are
indications that the people here are begin-

ning to have some perception of this; but vested interests have become strong under the present system, and the general absorption in money-making, causes people to be only too glad to get their charities performed by machinery, without occupying their time or distressing their feelings.

I see a great opening for doing good here. The mass is not so enormous as to swamp the unit, and it is possible sensibly to influence for good the future destinies of this young empire. The prospect of some such career will do much to reconcile me to a prolonged stay in the colony; for prolonged my stay must to all appearance be, if I hold to my resolution of not returning to England until I have achieved a competency. And to what end should I return sooner?

CHAPTER III.

A NEW WORLD INDEED.

From Herbert Ainslie's Journal.

I MET my host of the bush in Sydney
and promised to ride over and see him in
what he calls his town house. He was
quite right in saying I should have some
difficulty in finding it. It is where the
perpendicular cliffs subside into a little bay
opening on the broad Pacific, and is concealed by thick bush from the traveller on
the road. I got upon the sands without
discovering any habitation. At the end
of the curve the sea was breaking over
some hollow rocks with great noise, and

just out of its reach upon a sandstone ledge sat a lady in black, sketching. Tying my horse to a tree, I clambered over the rocks in order to inquire my way. Reaching the sketcher from behind, I had time to recognize in the drawing the same hand that so pleased me in the bush, ere she perceived me.

' The noise of the sea,' I said, apologetically, ' prevented my giving you warning of my approach.' But I rather thought that she was so absorbed in her work that she would have been equally unaware of it without the sea. As I spoke she looked up and slightly started. I know not what possessed me, but without a word I sat down on a ledge of rock near her feet. I can see now that it was a somewhat extraordinary action, and would have frightened most women out of their senses. But it seemed at the moment to be a matter of course ; and so she took it, for she did not appear the least surprised or disconcerted.

I said, 'I came to ask the way to your father's house. I little thought I should find an old friend here.'

'Why, how long have you known me?'

'Ever since I lost my way in the bush, and was hospitably entertained at Yarradale. By the help of a portrait I tried to fancy the author of all the pretty things there. And now that I see you, it seems as if I had known you all my life.'

She seemed to be repressing some emotion, and then said quietly, almost meditatively,

'I think I have known you longer than that; I mean before you were at Yarradale.'

'Indeed!' I exclaimed.

'Have you learnt to find the places at church yet?'

With an indescribable archness, and yet

with a manner indicating intense fear of causing pain, she said this.

'So it was you,' I exclaimed; 'you wore an impenetrable veil. But I feel that I should very soon have found it out if you had not mentioned it.'

She looked at me wonderingly and asked how.

'Partly by the voice, and the glimpse of your auburn hair. But mostly by a certain feeling of being perfectly at ease, so rare to me with a stranger, and which I then felt for the first time in my life, and now for the second. Do you know what I mean?'

'Perhaps.'

'What a savage you must have thought me.'

'You listened to the sermon.'

'Is that so rare?'

'Perhaps I ought not to say such a

thing, but I never observed any one, at least any of our squatters, for such I took you to be, listening to one before.'

'You know then that I am not a squatter?'

'Oh yes, my father told me—at least I guessed from his account of his visitor at Yarradale, that—— but I will show you the way to the house. He will be so glad to see you. He was delighted with your description of your travels. He has such a passion for adventure. You will cheer him, for he has felt much the loss of his only sister, who lived with us.'

How the stranger at church and her father's guest in the bush came to form one idea in her mind, and why she should be so confused, formed a mystery I was puzzling myself to solve when we reached the garden. Nor was it at all lessened when, after a most cordial greeting from Mr Travers whom we found there, he said to his daughter, 'Well, Mary, what do you think of the likeness now?' and she, muttering an inaudible reply, ran into the house and did not appear again until dinner-time.

There was the same perfect look of home about the place that had so much struck me at Yarradale. The same spirit and the same influence pervaded the house and its inmates, producing a feeling of intense and yet calm satisfaction and perfect contentment, which to me, who had been so long a stranger to the settled sensation of home and its certainties, was exquisitely delightful. And there was no mistaking its source; for as she sat at the table in the evening showing me her portfolio of drawings and paintings, it seemed to exhale from her very presence, shedding a dreamy blissfulness both upon her father, who sat apart watching her, and upon me; resembling, as nearly as I can describe it, a combination of the spirit that pervades Tennyson's 'Lotus-eaters,' with the condition known to mesmerists as that of being *en rapport.*

The drawings indicated a mind tinged with the loftiest romance, mingled with a deep sentiment of religiousness. There were Madonnas and Magdalens, angels and demigods, which, as I gazed upon them, excited in me a feeling of awe at the wondrous purity and power of the artist's soul. One face seemed to be a favourite of hers, for it recurred two or three times in the later drawings; the most striking instance being in an unfinished one of Don Quixote, and a painting, after Guido, of the Archangel's conquest of Satan. The Don was sitting on the root of an aged tree; his cloak, which had shielded him through the night, was cast aside, and his face was turned towards the east to watch for the rising sun, which already is dart-

ing one bright gleam into the forest depth,
lighting up his wan countenance, and revealing a face half joyous in the anticipation of high achievements, and half
saddened by the consciousness of isolation
and the world's scorn. It was a new
revelation to me of the knight-errant;
shorn entirely of the coarse and the ludicrous, and transfused into a high religious
symbol.

I was wondering where I had seen the
face of Michael before, so familiar to me,
when all at once I discovered that it was
a likeness of myself; so highly idealized
indeed as to be most appropriate to the
subject, but there was no mistaking the
type, though filled up more as nature perhaps intended mine to be, than with the
anxious weather-beaten aspect that I, alas,
am too conscious of having acquired.
The mystery was soon solved. The father after receiving me at Yarradale saw

the picture, and mentioned its resemblance to his benighted guest, and was told that it was suggested by a face she had once seen at church. It was by thus comparing notes she had come to the conclusion that the stranger at church and the guest in the bush were one and the same person.

I inquired why Satan appeared in the picture without a face, and learnt that he had once possessed a most diabolical countenance, but it happened to be so like a well-known colonial character that the gentle artist spoilt her picture rather than be liable to the charge of unkindness. She promised to carry out my suggestion, and represent him with the face crushed into the dust.

In my highly-strung state of feeling that evening, every trifle seemed to assume grand dimensions, and to cluster in a halo of charms around this Australian maiden. If such was the intense yet subdued delight of the evening, what shall I say of the singing glories of the morning? There was rain and gloom without, but her entrance into the breakfast-room seemed to bring with it a full bright burst of summer morn.

In her presence there is no need of any effort to seem, to be, or to understand. One seems to know all things by sympathy. There is a largeness of nature about her that entirely transcends the notion of what is called cleverness. For cleverness or adroitness implies effort, and that involves limitation. But with her there is nothing to suggest the idea of limitation. Power without effort, suppressed energy, concealment of method, economy of strength, are phrases that suggested themselves to me as I rode back to Sydney, endeavouring to comprehend the secret of her undefinable grace. In nothing does her peculiar character show

itself more than in her singing. It is intense without loudness, dramatic without
any approach to ranting. Her music does
not attempt to rival or outdo the words, but
only interprets and enforces them. Her
method is that of the magnifying-glass that
enlarges the object without being itself
obtrusive.

END OF VOL. II.

JOHN CHILDS AND SON, PRINTERS.

www.ingramcontent.com/pod-product-compliance
Lightning Source LLC
Chambersburg PA
CBHW020859020726
47497CB00005B/1477